## "I've Come About The Haunting Job," The Stranger Said, Stepping Into The Kitchen.

"You certainly look the part," Cassie told him. "Did my aunt explain what we want?"

"Someone to scare the bejammers out of your guests."

"It would be better if you were just to *shake* their bejammers a little, Mr — What did you say your name was?"

"Didn't. You can just call me Jonas. Capt. Jonas Middlebury."

"Well, what we need, Jonas, is for you to just show yourself. Not too often, because people won't believe it."

"They'll believe in me," Jonas stated, with a conviction Cassie found heartening. "I'll give you good value. Starting now."

"Starting now," Cassie agreed.

Yes. Things were definitely shaping up. This was going to be a very interesting vacation, she thought happily. Anything was possible, with a ghost in the kitchen—and the *very* attractive Dan Travis in an upstairs bedroom...

Dear Reader,

There's so much in store for you this month from Silhouette Desire! First, don't miss *Cowboys Don't Cry* by Anne McAllister. Not only is this a *Man of the Month*—it's also the first book in her new series. Look for the next two books in this series later in the year.

Another terrific mini-series, FROM HERE TO MATERNITY by Elizabeth Bevarly, also begins, with *A Dad Like Daniel*. These delightful stories about the joys of unexpected parenthood continue in September and November.

For those of you who like a touch of fantasy, take a look at Judith McWilliam's *Anything's Possible!* And the month is completed by Carol Devine's *A Man of the Land*, Audra Adams's *His Brother's Wife,* and *Truth or Dare* by Caroline Cross.

Happy reading!

*The Editors*

# Anything's Possible!

## JUDITH McWILLIAMS

*First published in Great Britain in 1995
by Silhouette Books, Eton House, 18-24 Paradise Road,
Richmond, Surrey TW9 1SR*

© Judith McWilliams 1995

*Silhouette, Silhouette Desire and Colophon are
Trade Marks of Harlequin Enterprises B.V.*

ISBN 0 373 05911 6

22-9507

*Made and printed in Great Britain*

## JUDITH McWILLIAMS

began to enjoy romances while in search of the proverbal "happily ever afters." But she always found herself rewriting the endings—and eventually the beginnings—of the books she read. Then her husband finally suggested that she write novels of her own, and she's been doing so ever since. An ex-teacher with four children, Judith has travelled the country extensively with her husband and has been greatly influenced by those experiences. But while not tending the garden or caring for her family, Judith does what she enjoys most—writing. She has also written under the name Charlotte Hines.

**Other Silhouette Books by Judith McWilliams**

*Silhouette Desire*

Reluctant Partners

# Prologue

—

"**N**ow, Millicent..."

"Don't you 'now Millicent' me, Jonas Middlebury!"

"But, Millicent—"

"No!" Millicent determinedly shook her head, sending wisps of golden hair flying around her pale face. "I have been listening to your excuses for one hundred and fifty years, and enough is enough."

"Not really, sweetlings," Jonas began placatingly. "I mean, I may have died a hundred and fifty years ago, but you've only been dead for fifty years or so."

"Eighty-one years," she corrected. "Eighty-one years, four months and seventeen days, and in all that time have you made the slightest effort to get into heaven? No," she rushed on when he opened his mouth. "And all you have to do is a good deed. Just one good deed."

"Done lots of good deeds in my time," Jonas muttered.

"Ha!" Millicent gave a ladylike sniff. "If you had done lots of good deeds when you were alive, Jonas Middlebury, you wouldn't be in this predicament now that you're dead!"

"It's not the good deed I object to," he continued doggedly. "It's the way that sanctimonious old puffguts at the gate told me I *had* to do it."

Millicent gasped. "Jonas Middlebury, you mind your tongue! That's an angel you're talking about, which is more than you're likely to ever be."

"I'll do the good deed, but in my own time," Jonas insisted. "I'm not about to be forced by no pen-pushing—"

"When?" Millicent demanded.

Jonas blinked. "When what?"

"When are you intending to do your good deed and get into heaven? At the rate you're going, the final judgment is a surer thing!"

"Now, sweetlings, you just don't understand how it goes against the grain for a man to be told what to do."

"I understand that I'm lonely." Millicent's lower lip trembled and her pale blue eyes looked huge through the tears that welled in them. "I understand that thanks to your selfishness I was cheated out of having a family and children."

"My selfishness!" Jonas' bushy black beard stiffened in outrage. "And was it my fault that I was drowned trying to earn a living for you in the only way I know how—whaling?"

"If you hadn't been drunk, you wouldn't have fallen overboard in the middle of the Atlantic," Millicent pointed out. "And if you hadn't fallen into the water, then poor Elias Simpson wouldn't have drowned himself trying to rescue you."

"Didn't ask the fool to come in after me," Jonas muttered. "Elias was always sticking his nose in where it wasn't wanted. He only did it because he wanted to hold it over my head afterward."

"I don't know about that, but I do know that Elias got into heaven the minute he died, while you are still wandering about trapped between heaven and earth. Or worse," she added ominously.

"Ain't never heard no talk about them wanting to send me to the other place," Jonas said testily.

Millicent stared into his beloved black eyes and felt a confusing mixture of anger, exasperation and love swirl through her. Jonas had been stalling for eighty-one years, and if she didn't force the issue, he'd probably stall for another eighty-one.

But if Jonas refused... Millicent felt a flash of blind panic. She might lose him altogether. She wouldn't even have these snatched bits of time to cherish. She drew a deep, steadying breath. It was a risk she was going to have to take. She simply couldn't go on like this. Jonas was no closer today to doing a good deed than he'd been when he'd died, a hundred and fifty years ago. He needed a shove. And it was up to her to give it to him.

Millicent took another deep breath and asked, "Do you love me?"

Jonas turned a bright red under his deep tan and tugged ineffectively at the collar of his rumpled white shirt. "Asked you to marry me, didn't I?"

"Yes, and drowned yourself before you could. And now you refuse to do a simple good deed so you can be with me. Do you know what I think?"

"Don't need to think," Jonas mumbled. "No good ever came of a woman thinking. It's not natural."

"I think you don't love me at all." Her voice broke at the pain of the thought. "I think I'm just a habit. A hundred-and-fifty-year-old habit."

"Millie, that's not true!" Jonas looked horrified at the charge. "I do! You know I do."

"Do what?" Millicent demanded.

"Love you, dammit!" he blurted out, then blushed a fiery red. "But there's no call for you to make me say it. Words aren't important. It's how a man acts that counts."

"Precisely!" Millicent nodded decisively. "And you consistently refused to act so that you can be with me."

"I told you, Millie, that's not it. I just don't like them letting Elias right into heaven when he was always such a meddling do-gooder and then telling me I wasn't quite the thing."

"If they haven't taken your point after a hundred and fifty years, they never will," she said with uncharacteristic tartness. "I'm telling you, Jonas, that you must either do your good deed and get into heaven or—"

"Or what?" Jonas demanded aggressively.

Millicent's lower lip trembled again and a tear trickled down her soft, pink cheek as a feeling of hopelessness washed over her. "Or I'll have to finally face the fact that I'm not important enough for you to make the effort." She forced the words out past her constricted throat muscles.

"Millie, no! Don't say that."

"I should have said it years ago," she murmured sadly.

Jonas stared for a long moment, her tormented expression tearing at him.

"All right," he said at last, capitulating. "I'll do it, but only because it means so much to you."

"Jonas!" She flung her arms around him in sudden, overwhelming joy. "You won't be sorry!"

"There, there." He patted her awkwardly on the shoulder, but made no effort to escape from her enthusiastic embrace. "No need to go overboard. That's how this whole mess started."

To his intense disappointment, she jumped to her feet and, moving to the edge of the cloud bank where they were sitting, peered down at the New Hampshire coastline below. "Are there any restrictions on your good deed?" she asked.

Jonas frowned, trying to remember what he'd been told. "No," he finally said. "It just has to be significant in the life of someone."

"That might present a problem," she said slowly. "What about the old lady who lives in our house now? Didn't you mention that she was having some troubles?"

Jonas nodded. "Since they built that new resort up the coast aways, she hasn't been able to rent out any of her rooms."

"Sounds to me like there's a good deed there," Millicent said.

Jonas absently scratched his beard. "Only way I can think to help her is to burn down the new resort so her clients'll come back, and I doubt if that sactimonious old pen pusher at the gate would accept that."

"No," Millicent agreed. "But there has to be another way."

Jonas frowned. "I could get her some money so that she doesn't need the income from the inn, but the only way to do that is to steal it, and while that might help her, it won't help me."

"There appears to be more to this good-deed business than first meets the eye," she said uncertainly.

"I could have told you that eighty-one years ago," Jonas said acerbically. "In fact, I rather think I did!"

"You promised," Millicent reminded him.

"And I'll do it. I just got to figure out what it is I'm doing."

"You'll think of something." Millicent smiled at him with a confidence that Jonas wished he could share. Now that he'd finally given in, he wanted to do his good deed and marry his Millicent. He watched with a nagging sense of loss as she slowly faded away.

Jonas got to his feet and absently brushed at the wisps of cloud clinging to his pants. He'd better get down to earth and see what he could work out. He heaved a disheartened sigh. If people thought living was hard, they ought to try dying!

# One

    "**W**hat you need is a gimmick, Aunt Hannah." Cassie Whitney absently scooped up a handful of fresh, red raspberries from the bowl on the kitchen table and began to munch them.

    "No, dear, what I need are paying guests. Even one or two would be nice."

    Hannah sighed despondently as she began to expertly shape the pastry for the raspberry tarts. "I feel so bad about Gertie. She depends on the money I pay her for cleaning the guests' rooms to supplement her social security, and if there're no guests..."

    Cassie eyed her aunt worriedly, beginning to fear that the situation was even worse than she'd originally thought when she'd arrived last night to find the normally bustling inn silent. It wasn't like Hannah to sound so discouraged. She had always been one of the most positive people Cassie had ever known. In fact, Cassie's father claimed that after forty-four years of reading *The Little Engine that Could* to her kindergarten classes, Hannah had been brainwashed into believing that anything *was* possible.

"And if the truth were told, dear, I feel sorry for myself, too." She gave Cassie a rueful smile. "I need the money the guests bring in. My pension is more than adequate for normal living expenses, but..." She glanced around the spacious, old-fashioned kitchen with affectionate resignation. "There's no denying China View is very expensive. The heating bills alone are horrendous, and something always seems to need fixing or painting or replacing. And the taxes..." Hannah shuddered.

"Are the taxes in arrears?" Cassie cut to the heart of the matter.

"Not exactly," Hannah hedged.

Cassie frowned as she considered the matter. "I would have thought you were either in arrears or you weren't."

"Well, you see, property taxes are paid in two installments. The first installment was due June first."

"And this is June twenty-second. So you're late."

"Technically, but the tax office always gives you a ninety-day grace period before they take any action. And I was able to make a partial payment," Hannah added.

"How much do we owe?"

"No, dear." Hannah shook her gray head emphatically. "How much do *I* owe. China View is my white elephant, not yours."

"It's the family's white elephant," Cassie insisted. "Whitneys have been living here forever."

"Only since 1844, when Jonas Middlebury died and left it to his fiancée, who was a distant relative of ours."

"How romantic." Cassie's blue-gray eyes softened dreamily. "To die tragically and leave the love of your life all your possessions."

"From all accounts, demon rum was the love of his life," Hannah said tartly. "He'd have made poor Millicent a terrible husband."

Cassie jumped at the sound of a thump coming from the pantry behind them. She turned and looked across the kitchen at the closed pantry door. "What was that?"

"Probably the wind blowing through the open window knocked something over," Hannah replied, dismissing the noise. "You've been living in New York City too long. You're nervous of your own shadow. Not only that, but you've lost weight." She frowned at Cassie's cheekbones, which were a shade too prominent beneath her creamy ivory skin. "You need fattening up."

"It's been a long, stressful winter in the advertising business." Cassie massively understated the case. "But also a very successful one. You are looking at Welton and Mitchell's newest vice president."

"Congratulations, dear." Hannah beamed with pride at Cassie's achievement.

"Thank you. And, since I got that promotion because I'm very good at selling things, why don't I use my expertise to sell China View to prospective guests? A month from now, when my vacation is over, you'll need my room for the surplus guests."

"Wouldn't it be a comfort to be booked full?" Hannah popped the tray of tarts into the oven. "But this is your vacation, dear. You're supposed to be resting."

"And I will," Cassie assured her. "But lying around doing nothing palls very quickly. I much prefer to have a project percolating in the back of my mind. It keeps me from getting bored.

"Now then," she went on briskly, "I think our first order of business had better be the taxes. I'll give you a check, and you can pay them."

"I just don't feel right taking money from you," Hannah said worriedly.

"Think of it as a temporary loan. I do earn an excellent salary."

"But I'm the adult and—"

Cassie laughed. "Aunt Hannah, it may have slipped your mind, but I'm thirty-four years old."

Hannah shook her head in disbelief. "It doesn't seem possible, but I guess you are. But even so..."

"Think of it as allowing me to invest in a piece of the family's history. Now, what we need is a plan of action." Cassie changed the subject before her aunt could think of any more objections. "Your business has dropped off because...?" She looked at her expectantly.

"Business has disappeared," Hannah corrected. "And it's because of that new resort they built four miles up the coast. I hear it's the last word in luxury. They have a swimming pool, plus the ocean at their doorstep and a fancy French chef."

Cassie munched on more raspberries as she considered the situation. "We don't want to compete with their strengths."

"We *can't* compete with their strengths!"

Cassie ignored the home truth. "They're offering an anonymous luxury that could be found anywhere. What we need to do is to push the local flavor of China View. This place is the essence of New Hampshire's whaling past, from the collection of scrimshaw in the living room to the widow's walk on the roof.

"Which brings us back to a gimmick." Cassie absently tucked a stray reddish brown curl behind her ear. "We need something to make China View stand out from the resort. Something to make it unique."

"Unique?" Hannah washed the flour off her hands as she considered the idea. "We could claim that the original owner brought back a treasure from one of his trips to the Orient and buried it on the grounds, and then drowned before he could retrieve it."

Cassie shook her head. "We'd have guests digging up every flower bed on the place."

"We could tell them that digging wasn't allowed?"

Cassie eyed her aunt with affectionate amusement. "That tactic may have been successful in your kindergarten classes, but I guarantee it doesn't work with adult greed. Anytime there's money to be had, and free money at that, the rules of civilized society seem to go by the board. No, we need an attraction that appeals to something safer than people's greed."

"You mean like their intellectual curiosity? They..." Hannah frowned at what sounded like a pan falling off a shelf in the pantry. "Oh, dear," she muttered. "I hope I haven't gotten mice again. I do so hate to kill the poor little things."

"That's it!" Cassie exclaimed, her eyes gleaming with sudden excitement. "It's perfect. It's even timely."

Hannah frowned in confusion. "Mice?"

"No, ghosts! Don't you see, Aunt Hannah? It's the perfect gimmick. We'll say that China View is haunted!"

"But that'll drive people away," Hannah protested.

"No, it won't," Cassie said with absolute conviction. "People love ghosts. I'll bet we'll be filled to capacity as soon as the news gets out."

"But how's it going to get out?"

"We're going to help it, of course." Cassie's soft pink lips lifted in a mischievous smile. "All we have to do is tell a few people that we saw what looked like a ghost, and the story'll be all over the coast by week's end. Maybe I can get Ed Veach at the newspaper to do a feature story on the sighting." Her eyes narrowed thoughtfully.

"Isn't that false advertising?" Hannah asked worriedly.

"Only if we actually claim that the inn has a ghost. And all I'm going to do is imply like crazy."

"But..."

"If you don't like the idea, Aunt Hannah, then of course I won't use it. But I really don't think it's wrong. It's not like we're charging more and promising a ghost."

"Our customers do get good value for their money," Hannah said slowly.

"And they'll have a great time trying to contact our ghost," Cassie added. "Do you know if there's ever been a hint of a ghost here at China View?"

"Not a murmur. I think ghosts are supposed to haunt places where violent deeds occurred, and nothing like that ever happened here."

"What *did* happen here?" Cassie asked.

"Not much. Jonas Middlebury built China View for his fiancée, Millicent Whitney, and drowned at sea right afterward. He left the house to Millicent, and she lived here until she died, shortly before the First World War. She willed it to her nephew, who was your grandfather, and when he died, he left it to me, since your papa had already moved to Boston. Nobody has ever even died here."

"Hmm, not much to work with." Cassie wrinkled her small, straight nose in disappointment. "Too bad we didn't have a more adventurous set of relatives. Jonas sounds the most interesting of the lot. How about if we claim that he's our specter?"

Hannah pushed her glasses back on her nose as she considered the idea. "He's probably our best choice. But what happens when no one ever sees him? People will stop coming, and I'll be right back where I was."

"What makes you think that they aren't going to see him?" The twinkle in Cassie's eyes deepened perceptively.

Hannah stared at her uncertainly. "Are they?"

"Yes," Cassie said slowly. "Not indiscriminate sightings, of course. Just an occasional glimpse."

"Moira Featheringham," Hannah unexpectedly said.

Cassie blinked. "Who?"

"An old friend of mine, dear. Moira is very active in our local theatrical group. She might know where we could hire someone to play the part of Jonas."

"Aunt Hannah, that's perfect!" Cassie beamed approvingly at her.

"Thank you, dear. I'll call Moira right now. Would you check the pantry for signs of mice and then keep an eye on the front desk for me? The only reservation I've had in weeks is supposed to arrive sometime late this morning."

"Glad to."

"And if you should need me for anything, dear, I'll be up in the attic. I want to make a start on going through the old trunks up there for the church rummage sale." With a preoccupied smile, Hannah disappeared up the back stairs.

Cassie finished off the last of the raspberries and then went to check the pantry. Opening the door, she stuck her head inside and glanced around. The window was closed, which left a mouse as the culprit. Stepping inside, she moved a few pans, looking for telltale droppings, but there was nothing to be seen.

Cassie frowned as she picked up an aluminum pie plate lying on the floor. It must have been stacked off balance and finally fallen, she decided as she carried it back to the kitchen. She set it down on the counter to be washed and then poured herself a mug of coffee, bringing it out to the tiny room off the lobby that served as an office. While she had the chance, she intended to go over the inn's books to try to get some idea of how her aunt stood financially.

Two hours later, Cassie had a much clearer picture of the situation, as well as a more optimistic view of the future. While it was true that China View was expensive to run, Hannah had resisted the impulse to borrow. With the exception of the taxes, she had no outstanding debts. If they could just lure some of her guests back, Hannah and Gertie would be fine.

Cassie looked up as she heard the sound of a car engine straining up the steep incline of the inn's driveway. Aunt Hannah's lone reservation? she wondered as she got to her feet. She straightened the front of her copper silk camp shirt and adjusted the thin leather belt on her white linen slacks before going to greet what she hoped was a paying customer.

She hurried through the inn's small lobby to the large window that faced the parking area in front. She peered out, but in the bright sunlight all she could see was a dark shape inside a white car. A rental car, she discovered, recognizing the sticker on the bumper.

Cassie instinctively leaned forward as the car door opened, curious as to what kind of guest they were about to get. Not the senior-citizen type China View normally attracted, she realized with sudden interest as a man slowly emerged from the car. This man was younger. Much younger. She studied the long, lean length of his legs, which were covered by a pair of tan cotton-twill pants, for an appreciative moment. Then her gaze skimmed upward over his flat stomach to linger speculatively on the width of his broad shoulders. Shoulders made even broader by the thick white cotton sweater he was wearing.

As she watched, he turned and, keeping one hand on the car door as if for support, studied the inn. The bright June sunlight poured over him, gilding his tanned skin to a shade of deep amber and adding a golden sheen to his honey brown hair. He looked aloof, remote and untouchable. As if he were a Greek god suddenly transported to earth.

Cassie shook her head in an effort to break the strange spell that the stranger's presence had enmeshed her in. It wasn't like her to react so fancifully to a man, she thought uneasily. Her years in advertising had long since taught her that physical looks counted for very little. They could be altered to create almost any image a person desired, just as they could mask virtually anything. It was the personality behind the looks that counted.

She watched as the man reached into the back seat of his car and pulled out a battered leather suitcase. He had a nice tush. In fact, he had a nice everything. Did everything include a wife? Her eyes narrowed consideringly. Somehow he didn't look like anybody's husband. He looked too... Cassie struggled to put a name to her impression. Unrestrained, she finally decided. He had an aura of being free and accountable to no one.

The sound of his footsteps on the weathered wooden boards of the front porch interrupted her speculations, and she retreated behind the reception desk.

The string of small bells above the front door gave off a silvery tinkle as the man pushed it open and stepped inside. His gaze swept around the small lobby assessingly, coming to an abrupt halt as he caught sight of Cassie. Leaving his suitcase just inside the door, he walked over to the reception desk and gave her a warm smile.

Even though Cassie was well used to the orthodontically perfect, gleaming white smiles of the male models she worked with, she was still taken aback. It wasn't that this man's smile was whiter or wider. It was that it was real, she realized. There was honest amusement in it. An amusement that was reflected in the tiny golden flecks that seemed to float in his dark brown eyes.

She swallowed against the sudden dryness in her mouth. She didn't know what this man had that was so potent, but whatever it was, she was certainly susceptible to it!

"This is China View, isn't it?" His deep voice vibrated through her confused thoughts. It fitted him exactly, she thought distractedly. Powerful, darkly intriguing and sexy as hell.

"Um, yes." She made a supreme effort to respond with her normal competence. "And you are...?"

"Dan Travis. I have a reservation."

Cassie checked her aunt's notation on the reservation sheet. "You're in Room Fourteen." She pushed the registration book toward him. "How long do you expect to be staying with us, Mr. Travis?"

"Dan, please." He scrawled his signature across the blank sheet. "And it rather depends."

"On what?" Cassie decided that the question wouldn't be out of line from an innkeeper.

Dan stared into her bright, curious eyes and wondered what she'd say if he told her the truth. The gleam of interest he was almost sure was flickering in her eyes would probably die, and she would avoid him like the plague. Or tell him to leave.

And he didn't want to leave. Not quite yet. His eyes swept over the mass of reddish brown curls that provided a vibrant frame for her classic features and lingered on the enticing curve of her lips. They looked so soft and velvety. What would they taste like? he wondered. Soft and sweet or tart and tantalizing?

She'd asked him a question; he pulled his wayward thoughts up short. If he didn't want to make her suspicious, he'd better say something.

His best bet would undoubtedly be to keep his answers as close to the truth as possible, he decided. That way he wouldn't have to remember a lot of lies.

"Business. I'm in insurance and, if something comes up that the office can't handle, I may have to leave. For the moment, I'm supposed to be taking it easy. I was in an accident." Bitter memory gave a painfully authentic edge to his voice. He'd never forget the whine of bullets whistling through the air. Or the dull thud they'd made as they'd slammed into the truck he'd been riding in. Or the terrified screams of the refugees in the back of that truck as the bullets had ripped through them. He clenched his teeth, trying to block out the memories.

Cassie glanced away from the raw pain burning in his eyes, feeling as if she had inadvertently intruded into something intensely personal. Had he lost someone he'd loved in the accident?

"So I decided to follow my doctor's advice and spend a few weeks lying around in the sun." Dan fought for an even tone.

"Doctors usually know best." Cassie heard her pronouncement with a feeling of disgust. How could she have just uttered such trite drivel, when what she'd really wanted was to say something to banish the pain that seemed to radiate from him? But he might well resent any personal comments from her, she conceded. And even if he didn't she still wouldn't know what to say. Somehow words seemed a scant defense against such palatable anguish. This was probably a classic example of Least Said, Soonest Mended, she told herself.

"My aunt may have explained when she took your reservation that the inn serves breakfast and dinner, but not lunch. Though if you ask in advance, a picnic lunch can be prepared for you. And we request a deposit of one night's stay," Cassie said, giving him her usual spiel.

"Certainly." He pulled an envelope out of his pants pocket and took out six one-hundred-dollar bills, dropping them on the counter. "Put that on my account."

Cassie stared blankly at the small pile of bills. No one paid for anything with cash these days. For one thing, it wasn't safe to be carrying that much money. There were too many people in the world only too eager to try to take it away from you....

She looked up, her eyes lingering speculatively on the hard thrust of his jaw. Dan Travis didn't look like he'd be an easy man to take advantage of. Unexpectedly, she shivered. Her gut reaction was that he'd deal with threats in a ruthless fashion.

"We do take credit cards," she offered.

He shrugged. "I've found that credit cards cause credit problems. I never use them."

"I see." Cassie picked up the bills, wondering why he was lying to her. That was a rental car he'd driven up in, and you couldn't rent a car without a credit card. So why would he use a credit card for his rental car and then pay cash for his room? It made no sense. Unless he didn't want whoever paid his bills to know that he'd been here. But why not? China View was about as innocuous a place as one could find. An eighteenth-century Puritan minister wouldn't find anything to complain about.

"Is cash a problem?" Dan asked.

"Umm, no," Cassie hastily disclaimed. "No, not at all." She scooped the bills up and shoved them into her pocket. "I was intending to go into town this afternoon anyway. I'll deposit it in the bank then."

"Is there a restaurant in town?"

"Uh-huh," Cassie murmured, debating whether to invite him along with her. He was definitely the most interesting thing that had happened on her vacation so far. And if past visits to China View were any indication, he was the most interesting thing that was likely to happen. On the other hand, she didn't want to give him the impression that she was in the habit of making a play for every personable male who appeared at the inn.

"I'll have to get directions from you," he said. "I missed breakfast, and I'll never last till dinner."

A hint to be asked along? Possibly. She would invite him to go with her, she finally decided. The worst thing that could happen would be for him to refuse. She'd survived men refusing her invitations in the past and undoubtedly would in the future.

"You're welcome to ride along with me if you like," she said casually. "I have an errand to run, but I always finish up by having coffee at the café."

"I'd love to." He gave her a sudden smile that sent a sparkle of anticipation through her. "If you can wait until I put my case in my room and make a phone call?"

"Sure. Just push nine for an outside line." Cassie handed him his key. "Number fourteen is at the top of the stairs, second door on the right. I'll meet you out front in half an hour."

She watched him out of the corner of her eye as he picked up his suitcase and began to slowly climb the stairs, obviously favoring his right leg.

Who did he want to call the minute he arrived? Cassie wondered as she went in search of her aunt, to tell her that her reservation had arrived and she was taking him into town with her.

She found Hannah in the attic, happily reliving the past as she sorted through the trunks that lined the walls. As Cassie had expected, she had no objections to her borrowing the car to go into town.

Cassie had just located her aunt's car keys on the kitchen counter when she heard a thump at the back door. She pocketed the keys and cautiously peered out the window over the kitchen sink. After twelve years of living in New York, being careful was second nature. Spying a man outside, she observed him carefully. Because of the way he was standing, she couldn't get a clear view of his face. All she could tell for certain was that he wasn't all that tall. Not much more than her own five-four.

Curious as to why he would have come to the back of the inn instead of the front, she opened the door. Her eyes widened as she studied the man standing on the stoop. He was wearing a rusty black suit of an antiquated design. Clutched in one of his large hands was a battered, black felt hat. Dusty boots covered his oversize feet, but it was his face that Cassie found fascinating. He had a full, black, bushy beard that almost totally obscured his features and piercing black eyes that snapped with some emotion.

"Well?" he demanded.

Impatience. Cassie identified the emotion with an inward sigh. She saw a lot of it in her line of work.

"Well what?" she shot back, refusing to be intimidated by someone who looked like he'd wandered out of a Broadway rehearsal. Broadway rehearsal? She examined the man more closely. He looked exactly like one of those old paintings of whaling captains hanging in the town library. She grinned happily at him. He was perfect. Absolutely perfect. Aunt Hannah's friend at the amateur theater group had done them proud. And on such short notice, too. Now, if only his command of acting was as good as his knowledge of period costumes, and he didn't demand a fortune for the impersonation. She hastily wiped the eager expression off her face.

"Won't you come in?" She moved aside.

"Thank 'ee." Jonas stepped into the kitchen. "I've come about the haunting job. I want it."

"You certainly look the part." Cassie gave credit where it was due. "Did Aunt Hannah's friend explain what we want?"

"Someone to scare the bejammers out of your guests."

"I think it would be better if you were just to *shake* their bejammers a little. I don't want to send anyone into shock."

Jonas shook his head in bemusement. "Beats me why anyone would want to be scared, even a little. But then there's no accounting for tastes and that's a fact."

"It's also one of the first premises of any advertising campaign. Now then, Mr.... What did you say your name was?"

"Didn't. You can just call me Jonas. Captain Jonas Middlebury."

Role immersion, Cassie thought in approval. "What we need, Jonas, is for you to put in an appearance most days for a few hours and judiciously allow yourself to be seen once. At most, twice. We don't want to saturate the market and destroy our credibility."

"Do you speak English, gal?" Jonas frowned at her. "Didn't understand a blamed thing you said. Ain't natural for a woman to talk like that."

"Don't get too far into the nineteenth century," Cassie said dryly. "Some modern woman is liable to strangle you. What I meant was that I don't want you to show yourself too often because people won't believe it."

"They'll believe in me," Jonas stated with a conviction Cassie found heartening. "I'll give you good value."

"What do you charge?"

"Hadn't thought about it." Jonas scratched his beard reflectively. "Haven't got much use for money, being a ghost and all." He shot a covetous glance at the freshly baked raspberry tarts sitting on the counter. "But now food, that's another matter."

"Ghosts don't eat." Cassie couldn't resist pointing out the flaw in his logic.

"Don't know about ghosts in general, but this ghost eats." He inched a little closer to the tarts.

Cassie found herself smiling at him. He was such an interesting mixture of belligerence and charm. "How about if we say five dollars an hour and all the food you can eat?"

"Deal." He sat down at the kitchen table, still staring at the pastries. "Starting now."

"Starting now," Cassie agreed, well pleased with their bargain. Jonas was absolutely perfect for the role. She couldn't have done better if the real Jonas Middlebury himself had materialized. She scooped a tart onto a plate and then, at his hopeful expression, added a second.

Yes. Things were definitely shaping up. This was going to be a very interesting vacation, she thought happily. Anything was possible with a ghost in the kitchen and Dan Travis in an upstairs bedroom.

# Two

***

**D**an unlocked the door to Room Fourteen and pushed his bag through with his foot, wincing when his leg protested the jerky movement.

He absently rubbed the healing flesh of his abused thigh as he looked around for the phone. He located it on the maple nightstand beside the king-size, white iron bedstead.

Gingerly, he sank down on the antique blue-and-white Irish-chain quilt, sighing when the pain in his leg eased. He wiggled slightly, finding the most comfortable position on the firm mattress and then reached for the phone. The sooner he let Harry know he'd arrived, the sooner he could find out exactly what his assignment in this godforsaken corner of the New Hampshire coast was.

To his surprise, Harry himself answered, and on the first ring. It was almost as if he'd been sitting at his desk waiting for the call.

"You all right, Travis?" Harry demanded.

Dan smiled at the impatient tone. He could almost see the man's bushy mustache quivering.

"Careful, you're starting to sound more like a mother hen than a hard-boiled newspaper editor," Dan said.

"I asked you if you were all right?" The volume of Harry's voice went up considerably. Dan shifted the phone to his other ear.

"Of course I'm all right. New York to New Hampshire is hardly a suicide run."

"I know, but..."

"But what?" Dan asked curiously. "Suppose you tell me exactly what this earth-shattering news story that only I could cover is?"

"Well... actually, I sent you to New Hampshire to *avoid* a story."

Dan frowned at the delicate floral prints hanging on the wall above the bed. "Harry, have you been drinking?"

"No, dammit! I've been thinking."

"Which might turn out to be every bit as dangerous in the long run," Dan said dryly.

"This is serious," Harry replied slowly. "You remember those articles you wrote on Buczek last month while you were still in the hospital?"

"Termite Buczek is not the kind of vermin one is likely to forget."

"Yeah, well, he's about to become even more memorable. The district attorney has decided to ask a federal grand jury for an indictment against him on racketeering charges. Directly as a result of your articles."

"Score one for our side."

Harry's sigh sounded across the phone line. "As long as that score doesn't come with a body count."

Dan's eyes narrowed thoughtfully. "Meaning exactly what?"

"Meaning that Buczek has aspirations. Aspirations that you have just put a nasty crimp in, and he is not a forgiving man. The word on the street is that he's put out a contract on you.'' Harry finally got to the point.

Dan sagged back against the mound of pillows at the head of the bed as a feeling of utter exhaustion washed over him. Ten years ago, even five, he'd have found the news that his articles had upset a crook to that extent exhilarating. He'd have relished the challenge of pitting his wits against a hired assassin. But now...

He shifted restlessly, wincing as a sharp pain shot up his thigh.

"Hell!" Harry exploded in frustration. "You haven't even healed from the last attempt on your life."

Dan's lips lifted in a grim caricature of a smile. "Ah, but there was nothing personal in that attack. They were simply firing at the UN convoy, and I just happened to be in the truck that took a direct hit." He snorted. "Nothing personal at all. I was just caught up in the generalized hatred that mankind spreads around."

"Careful, my friend. You're beginning to sound like a cynic."

He was beginning to feel like one, too, Dan thought uneasily. Somehow he was finding it increasingly difficult to care very much about the corruption and graft that he was continually uncovering. Exposing it didn't seem to help. It simply went on and on. Only the names and nationalities of the victims changed.

"Thanks for the warning, Harry," he finally said. "But as for hiding out up here, I have never run from a two-bit thug before, and I don't intend to start now."

"Think, man. The stories you normally write are about international upheavals. The people you expose can't get to you because by the time your stories appear in print you're out of their country. This is one of the few times you've done a story about corruption in the States."

"Yes, but—"

"No, dammit!" Harry interrupted harshly. "Last year I let Addison talk me out of his going into hiding until we could find out who was behind those death threats he was receiving. He swore he could take care of himself. They fished his body out of the East River two days later. I had to sit there at his funeral and listen while his wife and kids sobbed hysterically. Not again!" He was yelling. "Not ever again."

But that wouldn't be the case again. The unpalatable truth hit Dan with the force of a blow. There wasn't anyone Harry would have to comfort if Buczek killed him. There wasn't anyone who would weep hysterically over *his* coffin. A hard knot twisted painfully in his chest. There was not one single person in the whole world who would feel that his life had been shattered because he was dead. A numbing sensation began to spread through him. He had friends. Lots of friends who would be sad to think that he was no longer alive. But they would continue their own lives with barely an interruption and he would disappear into a void. As if he'd never lived. He felt stiff and chilled at the thought.

"This time we'll do what I think is right," Harry ordered. "China View is a perfect place for you to lie low while we try to find out whether Buczek is serious about hiring a hit man or merely bluffing to try to save face. Thank God you use your first name in your byline instead of the one everyone knows you by."

"God had nothing to do with it. It was my youthful sense of self-importance. Leland sounded so much more worthy of a Pulitzer Prize than just plain Dan." Dan grimaced at the memory. Seventeen years separated him from the young, idealistic college graduate he'd been then. Seventeen years filled with covering man's inhumanities to man. A lifetime of seeing things that no one should ever have to know even existed, let alone deal with. He swallowed at the metallic taste of hopelessness that coated his mouth.

Maybe it *was* time for a long vacation away from it all. And this place did have its compensations. An image of Cassie's bright face popped into his mind.

"You did remember to use cash, didn't you?" Harry demanded.

"Yes, Harry," Dan said soothingly. "I know all about tracing people through their credit-card purchases. And your contact was waiting at the airport in Portsmouth with the rental car just like you said he'd be."

"You be careful, you hear?" Harry thundered. "Get yourself killed and, by God, you're fired!"

Dan unexpectedly laughed. "I think firing me under those circumstances would come under the heading of the absolute, final straw. Call the minute you hear anything. Goodbye, Harry," he said and then hung up.

"Goodbye, Harry," Dan repeated as he got to his feet and walked over to the window. "Goodbye, New York. Goodbye, murder and mayhem." He took a deep breath of the salt-laden air drifting through the sheer white curtains. "And hello possibilities."

A smile unconsciously lifted his lips. The most intriguing possibility he'd seen so far was meeting him downstairs in— he glanced at his watch—right about now. He hurried toward the door, his movements awkward in his haste. She might think he'd changed his mind and not wait for him if he were late.

He found her sitting in a gorgeous vintage car in front of the inn.

"Where did you get a Packard in mint condition?" Dan asked reverently as he slowly circled the car, admiring it from every angle.

"My aunt bought it back in 1939."

"And she still has it?"

Cassie grinned at him. "It still works."

"I'm looking forward to meeting your aunt," he said as he got into the passenger seat.

Cassie shifted gears and accelerated down the steep driveway with the casualness of long practice. "Forget it," she said, having no trouble interpreting the covetous gleam in his eye. "My father has been trying to get his hands on this car for as long as I can remember, with absolutely no success. Although she did threaten to sell it to a collector in Portsmouth last year when they raised her collision rates again. What does your insurance company charge for vintage cars?"

Dan blinked. "What?"

"You said you were in insurance. What do you charge?"

"Um, we don't handle car insurance. We mostly do large commercial buildings and the like," he answered, improvising hastily. He should have claimed to be an author, he realized with the wisdom of hindsight. Something that didn't have a body of knowledge that he should know.

"I see," Cassie murmured, wondering whether to believe him or not. He could be telling the truth. Large commercial buildings did have insurance, so someone had to sell it to them. And it was possible that he wouldn't know much about the rest of the industry. So why did she have the nagging feeling that she was being lied to? And what would be his purpose? He didn't even know her. Maybe he was just an inept insurance man, she decided, glancing at him sideways as she turned onto the rugged coast road.

He was surreptitiously rubbing his palm over his right thigh, as if trying to massage a pain that was bone deep. A pain that he refused to give in to. Instead, he'd come with her. She would have expected a man with that kind of dogged determination to be a very knowledgeable insurance agent who knew all the ins and outs of the business.

But then, she didn't really know him, she reminded herself. Despite the inexplicable sense of recognition she'd felt when she'd first seen him, she didn't really know him. But perhaps she would by the time her vacation was over. The possibility lent a happy sense of anticipation to her thoughts.

The ride into Levington took only twenty minutes, despite the abysmal condition of the road.

"My God, don't they ever fix the potholes?" Dan gasped as she swerved perilously near the side of the road to avoid a particularly bad one. He peered out the window, his eyes widening as he calculated the sheer drop off the cliff to the shore below. "You were right to be concerned about insurance," he muttered. "Sooner or later you're going to need it. Or your survivors will."

"It's not that bad. No one's ever tumbled off that drop yet. At least, not sober they haven't," she amended. "One can't eliminate all of the dangers in life."

"No." The curtly spoken word held a bitterness out of all proportion to her casual comment. "And that, I take it, is the town of Levington?" Dan gestured toward the buildings that had came into view.

"Uh-huh. We'll stop by the newspaper office first." Cassie decided to start her rumors of ghost sightings there.

"Newspaper?" Dan frowned as she parked in front of a small, redbrick building, trying to decide what the chances of his being recognized by the staff were. Slim, he finally concluded. He had never used a picture with his stories and they'd be highly unlikely to connect Dan Travis who walked in off the street with Leland Travis, Pulitzer Prize winner. Besides, for him to suddenly refuse to go into the newspaper office would be bound to make Cassie suspicious of him. Something he didn't want to do.

"It's a pretty good little paper, even if it is only a weekly." Cassie climbed out of the car. "Ed Veach has run it for as long as I can remember."

"It must be nice to publish a weekly." Dan looked around curiously as he followed her into the building. "Just local news, with a minimum of carnage."

Cassie shot him a curious glance, wondering at the wistful tone in his voice, but before she could think of a way to phrase a question, she caught sight of Ed coming out of the storeroom in the back and hurried over to him.

"Ed, I have something I want to talk to you about," she said.

He eyed her suspiciously. "Whatever good cause you're selling raffle tickets for, I don't want any."

"I'm not selling anything," she told him.

Ed opened his eyes in mock surprise. "Will wonders never cease! You've actually come to *buy* some advertising?"

"No, not that either. Ed, this is Dan Travis, who's a guest at the inn. Dan, this cynic is Ed Veach."

Ed automatically shook the hand Dan held out. He stared intently into Dan's face for a long, puzzled moment, and then his mouth fell open. "Say, aren't you—"

"I'm Dan Travis, an insurance agent from New York City."

Cassie blinked, taken aback at the tone of Dan's voice. It had gone from casual pleasantness to... She peered uncertainly at him. For a moment he had sounded capable of... Of what? She scoffed at her imagination.

"Certainly, certainly. My mistake. Insurance, you say?" Ed continued with a knowing smile that made Cassie feel as if she'd missed something. "I'll bet you use lots of computers in the insurance business, don't you?"

"Yes," Dan said cautiously. "I would imagine most businesses these days are heavily into computers one way or another."

"You may not know this, Cassie—" Ed turned to her "—but we have a school bond issue coming up next month to raise money to buy computers for the kids."

"That's nice," Cassie murmured, having no interest whatsoever in it. She had more than enough to worry about with her aunt's vacancy problem.

"It occurs to me, Dan, that you might be willing to write a guest editorial for me," Ed said blandly. "Something along the lines of a businessman telling the voters why it would be a good idea to educate their children to compete in the twenty-first-century job market."

Cassie blinked, surprised at Ed's request. Her surprise grew at Dan's response. Instead of politely declining, as she would have expected, he gave Ed a rueful grin and muttered, "I'd love to."

"Good. Good." Ed rubbed his hands together in gleeful enthusiasm. "Now then—" he turned again to Cassie "—if you aren't selling and you aren't buying, why are you here?"

"I want your opinion." She tried to inject an uncertain note into her voice. "Being a newspaperman for as long as you have, I imagine you've seen it all, and the most extraordinary thing happened yesterday. I saw something on the back stairs, and then again in the attic." She shuddered and paused, giving the tension time to build.

"Spit it out, woman," Ed ordered.

"If I believed in ghosts," Cassie said hoarsely, "I'd say I saw the ghost of Jonas Middlebury."

"The ghost of—" Ed sputtered to a halt. "How do you know it was him?"

"Whatever I saw looked exactly like Jonas Middlebury was supposed to have looked, and since he died a hundred and fifty years ago..." Cassie allowed her voice to trail away suggestively.

"Sounds like a ghost to me," Dan stated calmly.

Ed gave him a scathing look and turned to Cassie. "And if the old geezer died a hundred and fifty years ago, then how do you know what he looked like?"

"They did have writing back then," Cassie said, hastily improvising. "And old Jonas wrote to his fiancée."

"You're saying the inn is haunted?" Ed demanded.

"Nope." Cassie was very careful not to make any false claims. "I'm merely saying that I saw something very strange that promptly disappeared. Since I don't believe in ghosts, I'm hoping that you have another explanation."

Dan studied Cassie's earnest expression, wondering what this was all about. She didn't seem to be the kind of nut who believed in the supernatural. His first impression of her—other than the fact that she was one very sexy lady—was that she was intelligent. But claiming to have seen ghosts was not exactly the hallmark of intelligence.

"Could you do a story on it and see if any of your readers have any ideas?" Cassie suggested with a hopeful look at Ed.

"You bring me a picture of your ghost, and I'll run it on the front page," Ed countered.

"If I can manage to get a photo, Ed Veach, I'll sell it to the highest bidder," Cassie shot back.

The editor chuckled. "That'll teach me, huh?" He turned to Dan. "You won't forget that editorial, will you?"

"No, I won't forget," Dan threw over his shoulder as he followed Cassie out of the newspaper office. "Is there really a ghost at China View?" he asked as he fell into step beside her.

"I saw something on the stairs." Cassie stopped in front of the bank. Pulling the deposit envelope out of her purse, she carefully stuffed it into the automatic deposit slot, cautiously checked to make sure it had gone down and then headed across the street to the café, intent on spreading the rumor further.

"And you think it was a ghost?" Dan persisted as he held the door for her.

"I have never believed in ghosts," she said honestly. "And I see no reason to change my mind simply because I saw something or *someone* who seemed to be able to disappear at will."

"Who disappeared?" Annie, the waitress, looked up from the cherry pie she was cutting. "Don't tell me we got us a little excitement in this place?"

"I don't think so." Cassie slipped onto one of the stools at the counter, figuring it would be easier to spread rumors from there than from one of the more-isolated booths in the back. "I'm sure it must have been my imagination."

"You?" Annie scoffed. "You're disgustingly level-headed."

"Her whole family is," Bill, seated farther down the counter, offered. "When I was in school with your father, Cassie, he had no more imagination than a garden slug."

"And your aunt Hannah has an explanation for everything," Jim, his elderly coffee-drinking crony added.

"Ain't that the truth," Annie muttered. "I still remember being in her kindergarten class."

"You and most of the town," Jim said. "What does Hannah have to say about what you saw?"

"Aunt Hannah doesn't believe in ghosts, either," Cassie said truthfully.

"What makes you think it was a ghost?" Annie demanded.

"I didn't say it was a ghost," Cassie said. "Just because I saw something on the stairs..."

"Something?" Jim peered at her. "This ain't no joke you're playing on us, is it, Cassie?"

"Absolutely not!" The conviction in Cassie's voice was unmistakable. It was certainly no game, she told herself, quieting her conscience. Her aunt's livelihood depended on this charade.

"What about you?" Bill asked Dan. "Have you seen this ghost she's talking about?"

Dan looked into Cassie's hopeful eyes and felt a curious twisting sensation in his chest. Despite his horror of manufacturing news, he couldn't quite divorce himself from whatever fantasy she was so carefully creating. And it wasn't as if it were really news, he decided, appeasing his conscience.

"Well, I'm not sure I actually saw anything. Not exactly," Dan said slowly.

"Well, what exactly?" Annie leaned over the counter.

"I heard something outside my room, but when I opened the door..." Dan paused.

"Yeah?" Jim demanded.

"I caught a glimpse of something out of the corner of my eye, and when I turned, it had disappeared. And there was this smell."

"What kind of smell?" Annie's faded blue eyes widened in delighted horror. "Like something out of the grave?"

Cassie blinked. This was getting out of hand. She certainly didn't want anyone associating China View with corpses.

Dan lowered his voice conspiratorially. "Of ambergris."

"Ambergris is what those whalers were after, isn't it?" Jim turned to Cassie in excitement. "And wasn't the man who built China View a whaling captain?"

"Yes, Jonas Middlebury was his name," she admitted. "But I'm sure there's a perfectly normal explanation for it. Like..." She purposefully looked uncertain.

"Cleaning supplies?" Dan offered.

"Yes, cleaning supplies." Cassie gave him a beaming smile that seemed to wrap around his chest and constrict his breathing.

"You were right." Dan nodded decisively. "There was a rational explanation."

"Ha!" Annie gave him a pitying look. "I've been cleaning more years than you been alive, and I tell you, there ain't no cleaning supply that smells like ambergris."

"Well, I, for one, prefer his explanation to ghosts," Cassie said.

Annie shivered happily. "Was he handsome?"

Cassie instinctively looked at Dan, and then realized Annie was referring to the supposed ghost. "Well, I didn't get a clear look at him, but he seemed to have a bushy black beard.''

"Sailing captains all had bushy beards," Bill offered.

Jim nodded in agreement. "Every picture I ever saw, they did. Cassie, you got yourself a ghost." He tossed some money down beside his empty plate and headed toward the door, with Bill hot on his heels. No doubt to spread the story, Cassie thought in satisfaction.

"Annie, I'll have a cup of coffee and a piece of that pie you're cutting, please," she said.

"Same for me, plus a hamburger," Dan ordered, rather surprised to realize he was hungry. It seemed so long since he'd thought about such mundane things as food.

"How can you be thinking about eating with a ghost haunting the inn?" Annie demanded.

"Nonsense," Cassie said. "Dan just gave us a perfectly adequate explanation for what he smelled, and I probably just saw..." She waved her hand vaguely.

"Ha!" Annie muttered as she poured the coffee, shoved a piece of pie in front of each of them and then hurried back to the kitchen to get the hamburger.

Cassie surreptitiously studied Dan out of the corner of her eye as she added cream and sugar to her coffee. He was meticulously eating the cherries out of his pie. Why had he backed up her story about a ghost? she wondered. He couldn't have really heard anything. She'd only just hired Jonas. The actor wouldn't have had time to get upstairs and be seen. Although adding the smell of ambergris was certainly a nice touch, she conceded.

"What does ambergris smell like?" she asked him curiously.

Dan gave her a wide grin. "Cleaning supplies?"

Annie bustled through the swinging doors from the kitchen, plopped a steaming hamburger and a gargantuan pile of fries in front of Dan and then turned to Cassie.

"Eppie says she don't believe in ghosts, and she wants to know if this is something to do with your job."

"I don't believe in ghosts, either, and I swear on a stack of Bibles that this has absolutely nothing to do with my job." Cassie put her hand over her heart. "I'm on vacation for the next month while I recharge my mental batteries."

"Ha! If you got a ghost out there at China View, it's more than likely he'll suck out all your mental energies."

"I think it's vampires who suck things out," Cassie said. "And I would definitely recognize a vampire. They smell like basements and dress in black and have long fangs."

Dan nodded in agreement. "That's why they absolutely never smile. Their teeth are a dead giveaway."

"You two can laugh now, but we'll see who has the last laugh," Annie said with ghoulish relish. "You let me know if anything else happens, promise?"

"Promise," Cassie agreed promptly, well pleased with the results of her afternoon's work. Unless she very much missed her guess, Jim and Bill were now over at the library spreading the story around the reading room, and Annie would tell everyone who came into the café. Probably with a few embellishments of her own.

"What job?" Dan asked curiously when Annie went to clean away Jim's and Bill's dirty dishes.

"What?" Cassie blinked in confusion.

"She wanted to know if the ghost sightings had something to do with your job. What job?"

"I'm in advertising," Cassie said.

"Advertising?" Dan repeated. His eyes wandered over her impossibly innocent looking features, lingering on the suppressed laughter in the back of her eyes and the upward tilt of her soft lips. She looked like a mischievous sprite. His glance dropped to her small breasts, outlined against her silk shirt. No, she looked like a very sexy, mischievous sprite, he amended. One whose secrets he couldn't wait to delve into.

"I'm at Welton and Mitchell in New York City. I'm a vice president," she couldn't resist adding at his skeptical expression.

He blinked in surprise at her disclosure. People, especially women, didn't get to be vice presidents of old established firms at her age unless they were very competent as well as very sharp. And very competent, very sharp people didn't spend their time spreading rumors about ghosts without a very good reason. So what was it? Finding out could be the most fun he'd had in years, he thought, feeling a stab of excitement ripple through him.

# Three

———

"You're sure you don't mind seeing to our guest this evening, dear?" Aunt Hannah asked uncertainly.

Mind being left alone with the most intriguing man she'd ever encountered at China View? Cassie thought as she smiled affectionately at her aunt.

"I don't like to leave you to cope all alone, but poor Jessie—you remember, she retired from teaching at the same time I did," Hannah added at Cassie's blank look. "She called while you were in town, and she sounded positively frantic. She got a registered letter this afternoon evicting her. It seems some developer from Portsmouth bought her apartment building and wants to tear it down, to build a fast-food restaurant of all things...." Hannah shook her graying hair in exasperation. "I'm helping Jessie organize a meeting of the other tenants tonight."

"I don't mind," Cassie assured her. "Dinner's all ready." She gestured toward the pots gently simmering on the stove. "All I have to do is serve it to him."

"Thank you, dear." Aunt Hannah gave her a warm hug and, with a militant expression that sat uneasily on her elderly face, marched out the kitchen door.

Cassie checked to make sure she hadn't spilled anything on the front of her jade silk shirtwaist dress and then went in search of Dan. She found him sitting in one of the white wicker rockers in the sun-room off the lobby. He was industriously rocking back and forth as he read the *Wall Street Journal.* It was as if he were too full of pent-up energy to sit quietly, Cassie thought as she studied him. He'd changed for dinner into a pale blue oxford shirt and a superbly cut Harris-tweed jacket that was slightly frayed at the cuffs.

"Would you like to eat now?" Cassie asked.

Dan looked up and his eyes met hers over the top of his paper. They seemed to gleam with all kinds of concealed emotions, emotions that lent an intoxicating promise to the evening.

"I'm starved." His eyes lingered on her mouth, adding intriguing shades of meaning to the simple phrase. "You will join me, won't you?" he asked as he got to his feet.

"Sure." Cassie accepted promptly, seeing no reason to be coy about preferring his company to eating alone. "Have a seat in the dining room, and I'll bring out dinner."

She hurried back into the kitchen and carefully loaded the serving tray. With any luck, he'd be so mellow from Aunt Hannah's delicious cooking—to say nothing of her own scintillating company—that by the time the evening was over, she'd know everything there was to know about him. Starting with why he hadn't used a credit card to register and why he'd agreed to write Ed's editorial.

Cassie paused, frowning at the sugar bowl as something suddenly occurred to her. How had Ed known that Dan could write anything, let alone a well-reasoned editorial? Writing was a finely honed skill—a skill that Ed had automatically assumed Dan possessed. Why?

Cassie thoughtfully added the creamer to the tray as she remembered the sly expression on Ed's face when he'd asked Dan to do it. Ed knew something about Dan. Or *thought* he knew something. But what? As an editor, Ed read all the dispatches from the news services. Could he have run across Dan's name or picture in a story?

She felt a momentary frisson of fear tighten the skin on her face before common sense doused it. If Ed knew something unsavory about Dan, he would have warned her. And he wouldn't have extorted a free editorial. He'd have called the police.

Picking up the tray, she shouldered open the kitchen door and entered the dining room. She automatically glanced around, looking for Dan, and found him bent over the huge fieldstone fireplace. He had taken off his jacket and was in the process of scattering her carefully laid fire with the brass poker.

Maybe he was an escaped pyromaniac, she thought ruefully as a shower of sparks disappeared up the chimney. She set the tray down on the table, and Dan glanced up at the sound.

"I love a fire," he said slowly. "Somehow its light seems to hold the horrors of the world at bay."

Cassie frowned at the bleak starkness of his expression. She wanted to erase it, but she didn't know the right words. Nor did she know if he would resent her attempt. So she did the only other thing she could think of and pretended not to notice.

"There." She finished unloading the tray and sat down, motioning him into the chair opposite her. "You have your choice of pot roast and veggies or veggies and pot roast."

"In that case, madam, I choose pot roast and vegetables. And coffee." He nodded toward the pot.

Cassie poured a cup and handed it to him. How could she direct the conversation along the lines she wanted? she wondered as she watched him stir cream and sugar into his coffee. A point-blank question would be worse than useless. Not only would he be unlikely to answer it, but it would put him on guard. It might even make him avoid her in the future.

The possibility sent a chill of loss through her. She didn't want him to avoid her. She wanted... What did she want from this comparative stranger who seemed so tantalizingly familiar? she asked herself. Companionship? Her eyes traced over his firm lips. No, she wanted more than that, she admitted honestly. She wanted to touch him. To kiss him. She squarely faced the compulsion that had been growing from the first moment she'd seen him.

"Why?" Dan asked.

Cassie blinked, for one moment thinking that he was asking her why she wanted to kiss him. Common sense came to her rescue. Dan Travis might be a fascinating man, but he wasn't clairvoyant.

"Why what?" she asked.

"Why is an advertising executive from New York City living in the wilds of New Hampshire spreading rumors about seeing ghosts?"

"I always spend my vacations with Aunt Hannah. And I happen to prefer the wilds of New Hampshire to the jungle of New York."

"But that still doesn't explain you telling people you've seen a ghost."

"I did not," Cassie insisted. "In fact, I quite clearly stated that not only did I not believe in ghosts, but that I was sure there was a reasonable explanation for what I saw."

Dan eyed her through the steam rising from his coffee cup, his expression unreadable. "Tell me more about your nonghost," he finally said.

Cassie frowned, wondering how it was that he was the one doing all the questioning when she'd been the one intending to. Maybe talking about Jonas would put Dan off guard, and she could slip in a few of her own questions, she de-cided.

"There's very little to tell," she said carefully. "I saw a man on the steps, and again in the attic, who looked like the description of Jonas Middlebury in Millicent's diaries. Not believing in ghosts, I was hoping that someone in town might have a logical explanation for what I saw."

"Maybe I'll see him?" Dan gave her a slow grin that made her very wary. He would not be an easy man to con.

"I wouldn't know. He didn't give me an itinerary of his hauntings. Do you have a weak heart?" she suddenly asked. He didn't look like he did, but then, looks could be deceptive.

"No, just a game leg." Dan instinctively rubbed his hand over his right thigh. "I think I'd like some of that pot roast." He purposefully changed the subject, and Cassie had no alternative but to go along with it.

She handed him the platter of pot roast, freezing as he reached for the plate and his rolled-up shirtsleeve stretched back over his forearm. Hastily she looked down at her own plate to hide her sense of shock. That was an almost-healed scar from a bullet wound on his arm! She was sure of it. Last fall she'd overseen an ad campaign to promote a vio-lent cops-and-robbers film, and the makeup man had had a wall full of photos of various bullet scars as examples to help him create fake scars on the characters. Cassie had spent the better part of three days listening to the man expound on what bullets did to human flesh and the difficulty of recre-ating that impact with makeup. There was no way she could ever mistake a bullet scar.

So why did Dan have one? Surreptitiously, she studied him. He was pouring gravy into the hole he'd made in his mound of mashed potatoes with a concentration she found endearing.

Cassie unconsciously relaxed. She didn't know why he'd been shot, but she would be willing to bet that he hadn't been doing anything illegal at the time. Maybe he was simply a careless hunter with very bad aim.

"You still haven't told me about your ghost," Dan persisted.

"Yes, I have. You simply didn't like what I told you. And since questions seem to be the order of the day—" she gave up on the subtle approach and opted for directness "—who did Ed think you were?"

"Beats me." Dan's shrug was a masterpiece of unconcern. "Ask him if you want to know."

"Why did you agree to write his editorial for him?" she persisted.

He grimaced. "It seemed like the neighborly thing to do, and it'll keep me from being bored. I'm not used to being idle."

That was possible, Cassie conceded. Dan seemed to be surrounded by a force field of energy. He could well be a workaholic type who needed something to keep him occupied. Although she could think of far more interesting things for him to do than to spend his time writing Ed's editorials, she thought dreamily.

"What are you thinking about?" he asked.

"About why people do things," she said obliquely.

"Personally, I've long since come to the conclusion that most people don't have any motivation. They simply react to events and then try to rationalize after the fact."

"You're oversimplifying," Cassie argued. "Most people have a goal. Something that drives them toward a certain end."

"Such as what made you tell Ed about the ghost?" He eyed her narrowly.

"Has anyone ever told you that persistence carried to extremes is no longer a virtue?" Cassie shot back.

Dan studied her for a long moment and then said, "What do you think is motivating me?"

Cassie stared at him. The skin around the corners of his bright eyes crinkled as if in humor. Or devilment, she thought with a spurt of excitement. Her gaze slipped lower to study the humorous quirk of his firm lips.

"Hunger for your dinner?" she asked.

"You're partially correct." He got to his feet and slowly walked around the table toward her. "Hunger is very definitely a major part of what is motivating me at the moment. But food isn't the source. You are."

"I are...am?" Her concentration faltered when he stopped scant inches from her. If she were to move ever so slightly, she would be touching him. She swallowed uneasily at the depth of the longing she felt to do exactly that. She tilted her head back and looked up at him. His mouth was curled in a sensuous smile that reflected her own longing, a fact that didn't help her crumbling composure.

"I want to kiss you." His voice deepened perceptibly. "Would you object if I did?"

Cassie stared at him, intrigued by his request. She was far more used to men who grabbed what they wanted—whether it was a thing or a person. To have a man actually ask for what he wanted was a novelty.

"No," she said slowly, "I wouldn't object."

"In that case..." He leaned forward and ever so gently pressed his lips to hers. A sudden surge of reaction shot through her, sending a flush of heat racing under her skin. The faint scent of his cologne drifted down into her lungs and then seeped into her mind, intensifying her reaction. His lips felt warm and firm and ever so faintly rough as he slowly rubbed them back and forth.

Cassie shivered, unconsciously clutching him. Her fingers dug into the firm muscles of his shoulder. She leaned forward, wanting more, much more than she was getting. She wanted to find out what it would be like if he were to wrap his arms around her and pull her up against him. If he were to press her body against his lean, muscled one.

Cassie blinked as a ringing sound filled her head. The telephone. Her mind automatically put a name to the sound. The telephone was ringing. She lifted her heavy lids and watched as Dan stepped back, a scowl on his face. That was exactly how she felt—as if she had been interrupted on the brink of some momentous discovery. But maybe it was for the best, she thought, a slither of reality chilling her sense of euphoria. She was getting in too deep, too fast with this man. She didn't know why she was so drawn to him. Or why he fascinated her so. And, more important, she didn't know how much of her fascination was reciprocated.

"Are we going to answer it?" His rueful question brought her back to earth with a thud. Her pride rebelled at the thought that he might think she was one of those vapid females thrown into a dither by a kiss. Because that was all it had been, she assured herself. A simple kiss. What hadn't been simple had been her reaction to it. That had been a masterpiece of complications.

"Excuse me," she muttered as she brushed past him, the skin on her arm tingling where it touched him. Cassie hurried out to the lobby, snatching up the phone on its sixth ring.

"China View Inn," she gasped.

"Connect me with Dan Travis' room, please." The polite request in no way disguised the underlying order. Cassie frowned at the vase of Madonna lilies sitting on the reception desk. Whoever her caller was, he was obviously used to being obeyed.

"Whom shall I tell him is calling?" Cassie asked, knowing it was really none of her business but curious all the same. The world would be a very boring place if everyone tended strictly to their own concerns, she thought, stifling her conscience.

"Work!" The man bit off the word, and Cassie gave up.

"Just a moment, please." She turned back toward the dining room to find that Dan had followed her and was now leaning against the end of the reception desk. Hoping he hadn't heard her questioning his caller, she held the phone out to him.

"It's for you," she said. "Someone from work. From the sound of his voice, something major you insure has just gone down the tubes."

Dan grimaced as he took the phone. "It's probably just Harry. He always sounds like his underwear's two sizes too small."

Cassie grinned at the apt description and retreated to the other end of the reception desk, her ears straining to hear what was being said.

Dan murmured something she couldn't quite catch and then said, "Just a minute, Harry. Let me go up to my room, where I won't be tying up the inn's phone-reservation line."

Turning to Cassie, he said, "Would you give me a couple of minutes to get upstairs and then transfer the call?"

"Of course." She gave the only response possible, wondering if his concern was for the inn's prospective business or about the fact that he might be overheard. Probably the latter, she decided as she watched him slowly climb the stairs, his right leg dragging slightly. Was there a partially healed bullet wound in his leg, too? she wondered.

She'd wait three minutes before she rang his room, she decided. That should give him ample time to get there.

Dan had almost reached his room when a high-pitched moan echoed eerily through the deserted hallway. For a split second he was catapulted back into the middle of the barbarous attack on the UN truck. He instinctively pressed his shaking body against the dubious protection of the wall and then cursed fluently when he realized what he was doing.

He forced himself to take a deep, cleansing breath, and then a second one as the first proved inadequate for banishing the horrific images that overwhelmed his thoughts. Images that seemed to lie in wait, ready to pop out and destroy his hard-won peace of mind at the slightest provocation. He rubbed trembling fingers over his forehead, which was damp with the cold clamminess of fear-induced sweat.

He made a monumental effort to focus his mind on a peaceful scene, as his therapist in the hospital had advised him to do. He closed his eyes and tried to call up an image of an empty field of wildflowers, but there was someone in his picture. Someone... An involuntary smile curved his lips as he realized that it was Cassie, and almost imperceptibly, his muscles started to relax. She was dancing gracefully through the daisies, her hands held out in welcome.

Feeling slightly better, as if he'd latched on to an anchor to a saner world, he started back down the hall, only to pause as he heard the moan again. It wasn't as startling the second time around. In fact, he wasn't even sure that it was human. Cats sometimes sounded like that. And probably a lot of other wildlife that could be found in the New Hampshire woods. He closed his eyes as he mentally tried to identify the sound.

It appeared to be coming from the window at the end of the hallway, Dan finally decided. He cautiously crept down the hall, not wanting to frighten the animal, and pulled aside the sheer, white cotton curtains, which were gently swaying in the evening breeze. Pushing the screen up, he stuck his head outside and then froze when he found himself staring into a pair of eyes that seemed to glow with yellow phosphorescence. Dan gulped as a pair of white teeth grinned evilly at him from the depths of a bushy black beard.

"Augh!" Jonas wailed, concluding his performance by slowly drifting toward the window. To his satisfaction, Dan instinctively jerked back inside.

"Not a bad job if I do say so myself," Jonas said, congratulating himself. "There's more to this spooking business than first meets the eye." He chuckled happily and floated up to the roof, leaving his victim sprawled on the floor just inside the window.

Dan rolled over on his back and peered up at the curtain billowing in the breeze above him—like a shroud. The chilling thought slithered through his mind. Like death . . . like . . . A ghost! The memory bubbled up through his confused thoughts. Cassie had spent the better part of the afternoon telling people about having seen a ghost. No. His lips lifted in a slow smile. She'd spent the afternoon telling people that she *hadn't* seen a ghost.

He clumsily got to his feet. This was undoubtedly the ghost that wasn't. He cautiously poked his head back out the window. To his disappointment, it had already vanished. Dan carefully looked around. The roof of the front porch was directly beneath the window, and it sloped to about eight feet above the ground. It would have been an easy matter for the ghost to crawl out through the open window, wait until he came along, scare the wits out of him and then, when he fell back inside, to jump off the roof and disappear. He could even have had a ladder propped up against the porch to facilitate his escape.

Dan grimaced at his own gullibility. If that moan hadn't catapulted him into the past, he never would have been so easily taken in. An anticipatory smile lit his eyes as he closed the window screen. "Just you wait, my ghostly friend," he muttered. "You won't find me such an easy mark the next time."

The sound of the phone ringing from his room reminded him of why he'd come upstairs in the first place, and he hurried to answer it.

"Travis here," he stated, waiting until he heard the click of Cassie hanging up before he added to that. From her questions at dinner, it was obvious she had her doubts about his cover story. And while he didn't think her suspicions would lead her to eavesdrop on a phone conversation, it wouldn't be the first time he'd been wrong about a person.

"Where the hell did they put you?" Harry barked out. "The attic? It's been five minutes."

Dan dropped down on the bed to take the pressure off his leg, which was beginning to ache. "Sorry, I was delayed by a ghost."

"A what?" Harry demanded.

Dan chuckled. "A ghost. And a very effective one it was, too. Scared the hell out of me."

"What's going on up there?" Harry's voice deepened. "Do you think Buczek's traced you there and is using the ghost as a cover?"

"No, I think our esteemed hostess is using the sighting of a ghost to drum up some publicity for the inn. It doesn't seem to be all that prosperous. In fact, I'm the only guest."

"Good. Let's keep it that way. I called to let you know that I've gotten confirmation of the rumor."

Dan sighed. He was damned sick and tired of being the target of every criminal and corrupt government official on five continents.

"Don't worry, Dan." Harry heard the sigh, but misunderstood the cause. "The paper won't let anything happen to you."

Sure, Dan thought sourly. It would look very bad if their Pulitzer Prize-winning reporter were to get his brains spattered out by a hired killer.

"Harry, what exactly have you found out?"

"An informant I trust called to say that one of Buczek's lieutenants offered a contract to his cousin to waste you."

Dan stared blindly at the tiny pink rosebuds running up the wallpaper in stripes as he tried to think. "Could your informant be simply hitting you up for money?" he finally asked.

"No, he didn't want any money. Said he was doing it strictly as a favor. Said his cousin told him that he didn't want any part of hitting someone as well known as you. Especially not for a lousy twenty thousand dollars."

Dan unexpectedly chuckled. "How nice to know one's worth."

Harry ignored him. "The lieutenant said he'd go with his second choice then."

"His second choice being?"

"He didn't say, and my informant didn't feel it would be healthy to show too much interest."

"Wise man. If he's got any sense, he'll distance himself permanently from the whole scene. Any rational person would."

"There's no call to be feeling sorry for yourself," Harry said bracingly.

"No call? It's only June and so far this year I've been shot full of holes and a penny-ante gangster has a contract out on me, and I shouldn't feel sorry for myself? Tell me, when do you think would be an appropriate time for me to indulge in a little self-pity?"

"This isn't like you, Dan." Harry sounded worried. "You've always ignored the dangers of your job."

"Harry, do you know how old I am?"

"What the hell does that have to do with it? It's your mind and your writing ability that defines you."

"I'll be forty next summer," Dan continued. "Forty years old and what do I have to show for it?"

"Financial security?" Harry offered. "Between what the paper pays you and all those books you've published, you must have millions stashed away. You never seem to spend it on anything."

"And what would I spend it on? A family?" Dan demanded. "I've never been in one place long enough to find a wife. Hell, I don't even have a car. I'm going to be forty years old, and all I have is a stock portfolio. Oh, and lest I forget, a hit man on my tail."

"This is not the time to indulge in a midlife crisis," Harry said testily.

"Yeah, you're right." Dan gave up trying to make him understand. Harry sat behind a desk all day long. To him, wars, famines and natural disasters were just words on paper. Not nightmares that poisoned his sleep and haunted his waking hours.

"Dan, I'm sending Justin Sloan up there to—"

"No!" Dan flatly vetoed the idea. "I don't have the slightest intention of allowing that—that smugly self-satisfied, egotistical, self-serving, Ivy League—"

"Now that's going too far," Harry protested. "I graduated from Columbia. For that matter, so did you. And whatever else Justin is, he is also the most competent man, besides you, that I've got. And he has a black belt in judo."

Dan snorted derisively. "That I don't find surprising. What I *do* find surprising is that he's willing to bury himself up here to wet-nurse me."

"Well…the fact is an ABC affiliate in California has been sounding me out about releasing him from his contract so that he can join their evening-news team."

"Good! Release him and get him out of our hair. Let Peter Jennings worry about him."

"I told Justin I would if he did this for me first."

"Great," Dan said in disgust. "I'll have the twit dogging my footsteps." And probably trying to make time with Cassie out of sheer boredom. A jagged shard of dark emotion flashed through him. Would Cassie be attracted to Justin's classic good looks and suave, sophisticated manner? Dan frowned, not finding the idea at all palatable.

"Quit bitching," Harry ordered. "As soon as this is over you can have your choice of covering the mess in Russia or the genocide in East Africa or—"

"Don't do me any favors!"

"Well, you can do me one. Get off this introspective kick you're on. Justin will be up tomorrow. Just to be on the safe side, I told him to pretend that he's never met you."

"Wonderful," Dan muttered. "Let's keep it that way." He hung up the phone with a thunk.

Leaning back against the soft mound of pillows, he stared blankly at the uneven slant of the ceiling. Was Harry right?

Was his massive discontent with his life nothing more than a temporary midlife crisis? He frowned. Maybe, but it seemed to him that for the first time in his life he was seeing the world clearly. Seeing it as it was and not as his idealism wanted it to be.

Although Harry did have a point about the money, he conceded. He didn't have to work to pay the bills. Not even if he were to decide to marry and raise a family. Cassie's laughing face unexpectedly popped into his mind.

Dan squinted at the blue Tiffany lampshade on the bedside table. No, he didn't have to work to pay the bills, but he might well have to work to preserve his sanity. He wasn't the kind of man who would be happy doing nothing day after day. He needed something to occupy his time, something he believed in. Something that gave a structure to his time. But if not reporting, then what? He closed his eyes to think and drifted off into an exhausted sleep.

"Jonas Middlebury, I saw what you did." Millicent gingerly sat down beside him on the roof, being careful not to brush up against the sooty chimney. "And after you promised that you were going to try to get into heaven!" She eyed him reproachfully, her large blue eyes filling with tears.

"If that isn't just like a woman!" Jonas said in exasperation. "First they tell you to do something, and then, when you do it, they bellyache about it."

"I am not bellyaching!" Millicent sniffed indignantly. "And I most certainly didn't tell you to frighten some poor stranger to death."

"Bah, he wasn't all that frightened. Leastwise, he wasn't after the first shock. Got to work on my technique," he mused, and then, at Millicent's outraged gasp, complained, "You told me to help the old lady who lives in our house, didn't you?"

"Yes, but I don't think scaring away her customers is going to help her into anything other than an early grave!"

"Well, I sure hope she rests easier in hers than I'm getting to in mine!" Jonas shot back. "For your information, her niece hired me to haunt the place."

Millicent stared at him in shock. "She never!"

"Did so. She seems to think that my haunting will bring guests to the inn, not drive them away. Can't see it myself, but then there's no denying the world is a mighty strange place these days. Kinda makes a fella glad to be dead. Leastwise, it would if'n I could get into heaven."

"Well...if she asked you to do it and she thinks it will help...I guess it ought to fulfill all the requirements," Millicent finally said.

"I sure hope so," Jonas muttered, "because this good-deed business is mighty wearing."

# Four

---

Cassie peered into the dining room, but it was empty, as the sun-room had been. A sharp stab of disappointment dampened her initial pleasure in the gorgeous morning. She wanted to see Dan, to talk to him. To make sure he was the same as she remembered him. The memory of his brief kiss at dinner last night had been her last waking thought, painting her dreams with erotic fantasies.

A flicker of uncertainty over her preoccupation with the inn's only guest seeped into her mind, partially deflating her sense of anticipation. It was one thing to indulge in a harmless vacation romance, she told herself, but quite another to allow that romance to displace the things she should be worrying about, such as the inn's lack of guests.

So why was she so preoccupied with him? She tried to analyze her compulsive reaction as she slowly walked to the kitchen. Normally, she wasn't an impulsive person, or emotional. All her past relationships with men, in fact, had tended to fall into the same pattern. First she was drawn to them mentally, and as she got to know them over time, that attraction grew to include physical desire. Never before had she looked at a man and felt a compulsion to touch him. To kiss him. To make love to him.

She grimaced in frustration. Why was Dan so different? The question nagged at her, but she couldn't answer it any more than she could deny the basic compulsion that gripped her.

Time was what she needed, she finally decided. Time to see if what she felt would dissipate or blossom into something else. And she wasn't even sure which alternative she preferred.

She pushed open the kitchen door.

"Good morning, dear." Aunt Hannah looked up from the cake she was icing. "I like your dress. That shade of cyan makes your eyes more blue than gray."

"Thank you," Cassie murmured as she surreptitiously glanced over at the sink. To her disappointment, there were several freshly washed dishes drying on the counter. Had Dan already had his breakfast? She glanced at the clock. It was nine. Not very late for someone on vacation. Unless the plates belonged to Jonas?

"Aunt Hannah, did a man named Jonas come by this morning?"

Hannah chuckled. "He was at the kitchen door five minutes after I put the coffeepot on. He explained that you'd hired him and then wolfed down six of my cinnamon rolls and most of a pot of coffee. I had to make more for Mr. Travis."

"Dan's already had his breakfast?"

"Yes, dear, over an hour ago."

"Oh? I didn't see him as I came through the front of the inn." Cassie tried to sound casual.

"He mentioned something about going for a walk along the beach." Hannah shook her head. "Poor man. His leg was obviously bothering him, but he said that walking was part of his therapy. Cars are so dangerous these days."

And guns were still more dangerous, Cassie thought, recalling the fresh bullet scar on his forearm. Maybe he was a cop who'd been shot by a criminal? She frowned. Somehow, Dan didn't seem like a cop. It wasn't anything she could put her finger on, but he just didn't fit the role.

"Don't look so worried, dear." Hannah misunderstood her frown. "He won't come to any grief on the beach. And if he hasn't returned by the time I get back, I'll help you look for him."

"Where are you going?" Cassie asked.

"Into town." Hannah washed the icing off her hands. "I promised the education committee I'd give them some ideas on how to get parents more involved in the schools."

Cassie smiled at her. "I don't know why you ever retired, Aunt Hannah. You're always over at the school anyway."

Hannah set her gray felt hat on her head and anchored it with a lethal-looking pearl stickpin. "Yes, but now I only do the parts that I like. You're sure you don't mind keeping an eye on things for me? Gertie won't be in until after lunch, but I don't absolutely have to go this morning."

"Nonsense, I'm more than capable of registering the hordes of guests that will undoubtedly come." She kissed Hannah's soft cheek.

To say nothing of taking very good care of one particular guest, Cassie thought as she walked her aunt out to the garage. She waved goodbye as Hannah drove off and then went back to the kitchen. Pouring herself a cup of coffee, she idly sipped it as she mentally arranged her day.

If Dan wanted to exercise his leg... A flicker of excitement darted through her mind. She had far more provocative ideas for exercising than trudging up a sandy beach and getting sunburned.

The sound of a car pulling into the parking lot in front of the inn interrupted her thoughts, and she went to see if her aunt had forgotten something. But it wasn't the ancient Packard returning. It was a white rental car arriving. A twin to Dan's.

Cassie peered out the front window beside the door, squinting in the strong sunlight as she tried to see who it was. A man driving by himself. A customer, she hoped.

She hastily arranged her hair with her fingers, twitched her belt into place, pinned on a professional smile and hurried behind the reception desk. She watched as a man in his early thirties strode into the lobby. He paused just inside the door and glanced around with an arrogance that immediately set her teeth on edge.

"You there." He frowned impatiently at Cassie, and she stifled the impulse to say something rude.

"Yes?" she asked crisply.

"This is China View Guest House, isn't it?" His arrogance developed a tinge of uncertainty as he came closer and got a good look at the dress she was wearing. Cassie didn't have the slightest doubt that, unlike her aunt, who had noticed only the color, this man knew exactly which designer had created it as well as how much she'd paid for it. Clearly, her outfit didn't match his preconceived notions of how an innkeeper in New Hampshire was supposed to look.

"So the sign outside says." Cassie couldn't resist the small gibe. What was the matter with her this week? she wondered uneasily. Every man she met seemed to provoke an uncharacteristic reaction in her. This time it was negative.

"I wish to register." He pulled his wallet out of the inside pocket of his custom-tailored navy blazer.

Italian hand-tooled leather and very expensive. Cassie recognized the maker.

She frowned as he pulled five one-hundred-dollar bills out of his wallet and dropped them on the counter.

"We do take all the major credit cards," she offered, wondering what was going on. People never paid for their rooms with cash. And yet, within the space of a few days, she had two guests who were flinging hundred-dollar bills around as if they were printing them on the side.

"I never use credit cards," he said.

Liar, Cassie thought as she handed him the registration book to sign. That rental car out front hadn't been paid for with cash. He had to have used a credit card for it. Just as Dan had. And like Dan, he'd lied about it. Maybe eschewing credit cards was the latest male thing? she wondered in exasperation as she stashed the bills in the strongbox under the counter.

"You're in Room Sixteen. It's the first door on the right at the top of the stairs, Mr...." She leaned over to read his name out of the registration book. "Smith?" She bit back a giggle just in time. She'd bet every penny of her last bonus that his name was no more Smith than hers was. But why use an alias? she wondered as she handed him the key. Maybe he was meeting a woman for a wild fling and wanted anonymity? She hoped so. It would mean renting another room.

Smith tossed his car keys onto the counter. "My luggage is in the trunk. Have it sent up immediately," he ordered as he headed toward the stairs.

Cassie stared at the silver keys and slowly counted to ten. Aunt Hannah needed the money, she reminded herself, and lugging his bags wouldn't hurt her.

She snatched up his keys and went outside. She paused on the porch steps and looked up and down the beach for Dan. She couldn't see him. Worriedly, she bit her lip. Supposing his bad leg had given out? Supposing he'd fallen and couldn't make his way back? Suppose you quit giving such free rein to your imagination, she ordered herself. Dan Travis was a grown man who undoubtedly knew what he was physically capable of.

Determinedly putting him out of her mind, she unlocked the trunk of Smith's rental car and yanked out his three oversize bags. She hadn't brought this much for a month's stay, she thought in annoyance. She was maneuvering them through the front door when Jonas' voice startled her, and she dropped one of the cases.

"Jonas, I swear I'm going to tie a bell around you. It's not natural the way you sneak up on people."

Jonas cackled happily. "It is if'n you're a ghost."

"Be careful you don't get too far into your role," she said dryly. "You're liable to get typecast. And be careful you aren't overheard talking to me. We have a new guest for you to try your wiles on."

"I know. I saw him when he got out of the car. Straightening his hair he was, just like a gal." Jonas snorted. "I'd like to raise it a little for him."

"Feel free," Cassie said encouragingly. "He paid in advance."

"Let me have those." Jonas grabbed the bags out of her hands. "Don't know what the world is coming to when a grown man leaves his lifting for a woman."

"He might see you," Cassie objected. "We don't want to blow your cover."

"Nah, his kind never see what's not in the mirror. But if'n you're worried, you go first and make sure he isn't in the hall."

"Thanks. I appreciate it."

"Enough to give me a piece of that cake your aunt was making?" Jonas gave her a hopeful look.

"Sure. You can have anything you can find. I'll even give you the tip. Provided he gives me one," she qualified.

"Cake'll be plenty. And maybe another cup of that delicious coffee." He started up the stairs.

Cassie hurried around him. She paused at the landing and, when she didn't hear anything, softly crept up the last few steps and peered toward Smith's door. She froze when she caught a glimpse of movement farther down the hallway. The room he was coming out of wasn't the one she'd assigned him, she realized. It was Dan's room. She frowned. Why would Smith have gone into Dan's room?

Deciding that the only way to find out would be to ask, Cassie stepped into the hallway and said, "Are you having a problem finding your room, Mr. Smith?"

Smith jerked around at the sound of her voice and stared blankly at her.

Cassie could almost see the wheels turning in his head as he tried to decide what to say. She didn't have the slightest doubt that the truth was not one of the options he considered.

"I forgot my glasses," he finally said. "And being nearsighted, I confused the numbers on the doors. But once inside I realized that the room was occupied and I'd made a mistake." He gave her a practiced, gleaming smile that she had no doubt was supposed to reduce the poor little provincial to tongue-tied shyness.

"I see," Cassie murmured, not believing for one moment that he'd ever spoil his classic profile with glasses. Not him. Contacts, yes. Glasses, no. "How unfortunate. I'll find a nice bright picture and tape it to your door so that it doesn't happen again."

"Oh, it won't be necessary," he assured her. "I'm just so glad that I didn't startle whoever is staying there. Do you know where he is?"

"No," Cassie lied. She had no intention of telling Smith anything until she knew a little more about him.

"I guess this is where I belong." He opened the door to number sixteen and, edging inside, hurriedly closed it behind him.

Cassie turned back to get the bags from Jonas, but Jonas had already disappeared. Careless of their highly polished leather surfaces, she dragged Smith's suitcases down the hall and left them in front of his door.

She wanted to see Dan, to tell him what she'd seen and find out if he knew this Smith. Or knew of him. Cassie opened the window screen at the end of the hallway, stuck her head out and looked toward the beach. A shiver of pleasure danced through her as she caught sight of Dan trudging toward the house. Her sense of pleasure diminished somewhat as she watched his uneven progress across the hard-packed sand. The way he was dragging his leg, he looked awkward and tired. And alone. So very alone. She studied his halting movements, silhouetted against the endless swell of the ocean.

Driven by a compulsion she didn't understand but couldn't resist, she slammed the screen closed and hurried downstairs to meet him. She caught up with him just as he was entering her aunt's herb garden beside the house.

Eagerly, her eyes skimmed over him. His skin had a healthy glow to it, his hair was enticingly wind tossed and his eyes were bright with intelligence and other less easily defined emotions.

"Good morning," she offered, suddenly feeling shy.

"Definitely a good morning." He smiled at her, and his smile seemed to envelope her in a warm sense of welcome. His obvious pleasure at her appearance melted her momentary uncertainty, and she happily fell into step beside him.

"Any chance for a cup of coffee?" he asked.

"Go around to the front porch and I'll bring you a cup," she said, not wanting him to enter the kitchen and find Jonas.

"I don't mind drinking it in the kitchen."

"It would be much more pleasant on the front porch in the fresh air," Cassie improvised, suddenly feeling a reluctant kinship with Smith. Spur-of-the-moment lying wasn't all that easy to do. "Meet you in five minutes," she said, and she hurried around to the back of the house, not giving him time to object.

To her relief, Jonas was not in the kitchen. Nor was a quarter of the cake her aunt had baked. Cassie grinned ruefully, wondering how long it would take their "ghost" to fill up his hollow leg.

She paused in the middle of pouring out the coffee to wonder suddenly how Jonas had left the inn. He hadn't driven away, because she hadn't seen or heard any car except Smith's and her aunt's. And there was no place for him to park one along the narrow, winding road that led from the coast road to the inn. He probably had a bicycle, she finally decided.

She quickly finished filling the mugs, added sugar and cream and hurried through the inn to the front porch. She found Dan slouched in a wicker rocker, his injured leg stretched out in front of him, his eyes closed. As she approached, he opened his eyes and straightened up. He pushed up one sleeve of his white cotton sweater, but it promptly fell back down.

"I wanted to talk to you about what happened last night when I went up to take my phone call," he said as he reached for one of the mugs.

"Oh?" Cassie asked, suddenly wary. She had assumed when he hadn't returned to finish his dinner, and when there hadn't been any noise coming from his room when she'd casually wandered by, that he had fallen asleep. But perhaps he'd been doing something?

Dan took a sip of his coffee, studying her over the rim with a narrow-eyed intensity that put her in mind of her boss when he was trying to decide what approach to use to get her to take on yet one more project she didn't have time for.

"As I was going to my bedroom, I heard a sound outside that window at the end of the hall."

"Really?" Cassie gave him her best I-have-no-idea-what-you're-talking-about look.

"Yes, really," he repeated dryly. "I looked out and do you know what I saw?"

"No, but I can see that you're dying to tell me."

"I saw your ghost."

"He isn't *my* anything," Cassie protested. "I said I saw something, but I also said that I didn't believe in ghosts."

"Neither do I, but if I did, I'd sure believe in your captain."

"I don't know why you keep calling him mine," Cassie protested. "I've already told you I don't think he exists."

"Now why don't I believe you?"

"You're a cynic?" she teased.

"What's the old saying? A cynic is a person who knows the price of everything and the value of nothing?"

"I don't know. But I do know that it's far too nice a morning for such a morbid discussion," she protested. "I'd rather talk about our latest guest and the fact that when I went upstairs a few minutes ago I found him coming out of your room. He said he'd mistaken his way." She snorted in disgust at such a lame excuse.

"And what did your inept burglar look like?" Dan asked with far less interest than she would have expected. If someone had told her they'd seen a stranger coming out of *her* room, she'd have been upset and annoyed. She wouldn't be casually asking for a description.

"What does it matter what he looks like, for heaven's sake?" she demanded.

"Some housebreakers are more sinister than others. Describe him."

"I'd use him in upper-income campaigns," she said slowly. "But stills. I'd be afraid to let him open his mouth for fear that his disdain for the rest of us mortals might damage the customers' view of the product."

Dan stared at her. "What?"

"You wanted a description. That was how he struck me. As a self-centered, self-satisfied man who puts a great deal of emphasis on outward appearances."

That sounded like Justin Sloan, all right. Dan unconsciously relaxed. Cassie hadn't been taken in at all by his
pretty-boy exterior. From what he'd seen, that made her a
minority of one. No, not quite, Dan suddenly realized. The
secretaries in the newspaper office couldn't stand him, either.

But Justin couldn't be the only smugly self-satisfied twit
running around, and he'd better make sure it was he. Especially if Harry was right and Buczek really had put out a
contract on him.

"Give me a description that I can use to recognize him if
I run into him in the dining room," Dan ordered.

"Well, he's about six-two, with classic features, a nose
that has probably been bobbed, a square jaw with a cleft,
tanned skin, perfectly capped teeth, brown hair treated to
simulate sun bleaching, very expensive Saville Row tailor-
ing more suitable for a weekend at Ascot than for a small
inn in New Hampshire, a thirty-odd-thousand-dollar watch,
hand-sewn brown leather loafers and a gold-and-onyx sig-
net ring. I didn't notice the insignia," she added.

Dan blinked, taken aback at the completeness of the description. He'd worked with seasoned reporters who didn't
see that much. "It must have been the only thing you didn't
notice," he finally said.

"I am in advertising," she said. "And a great deal of advertising is creating the right impression. Smith is a type I'm
familiar with. What I can't figure out is why he's here and
what he was doing in your room."

Dan shrugged. Now that he knew it really was Justin
Sloan who'd checked in and that he was using the name of
Smith—he mentally shook his head at the idiocy of Sloan's
choice of aliases—he had no further interest in him. Nor did
he want Cassie to devote any of her time to him.

"Forget Smith or Jones or whoever he is," Dan ordered.
"I need a copy of Ed Veach's newspaper. Your aunt says she

already threw out this week's edition, but she thought there might be some old issues up in the attic.''

"Then perhaps you should discuss the matter with her," Cassie snapped, annoyed at his refusal to take Smith seriously. There was something wrong about their latest guest. She could almost taste it. So why couldn't Dan?

He gave her a shocked look. "I couldn't ask that dear old lady to go rooting around in an attic."

"But I take it you're about to ask her niece to do it?" She eyed him narrowly.

"Her much-younger niece."

"But her not-naive niece. I know full well when I'm being diverted. To say nothing of being patronized!"

"I am not patronizing you," Dan said flatly. The very hardness of his voice lent credence to what he was saying. "I simply find Smith of no interest whatsoever. But I can see that I'm going to have to work on my diversionary tactics."

He carefully set his half-empty coffee mug on the floor and leaned toward her. Cassie's breath shortened as she watched him come closer, close enough so that she could touch him. Close enough for her to run her fingertips over his lean cheeks. Close enough that if she were to shift forward even slightly, she could press her lips to his.

She took a shallow breath and ran the tip of her tongue over her suddenly dry lips.

"Now, I haven't had a great deal of experience at diverting women, you understand." Dan's voice dropped to a husky murmur that played havoc with her thought processes.

"You haven't?" she muttered, refusing to believe that he could be having this much effect on her without having polished his technique on other women. A lot of other women.

"No, I haven't." A bleak expression replaced the teasing glint in his eyes, and Cassie instinctively reached out to comfort him. Her hand curved around his cheek and a shiver chased up her arm as the faint raspy texture of his cleanly shaven skin scraped across her palm.

Cassie closed her eyes and tried to think. What was she doing? Comforting a man because he didn't have a great deal of experience at diverting other women? That was nuts. She opened her eyes and found herself staring into his eyes, which blazed with emotion. An emotion that seemed to reach out and pull her closer to him.

"But," Dan whispered softly, "I'm a great improviser."

"How nice," she murmured, her gaze focused on the enticing movements of his lips. The urge to explore their texture was a driving need. A need she could think of no rational reason to deny herself. Dan might be trying to divert her, but she was more than willing to be diverted if the reward was to be able to kiss him again.

She slipped her hand around the back of his neck, shuddering as the prickly ends of his hair stabbed her fingers. Her grip tightened as she tugged him toward her.

It was all the encouragement Dan needed. His hands closed around her shoulders and he pulled her up against him with a rough hunger that she found far more appealing than the most practiced technique. The scent of his cologne mingled with the salty tang of his skin and seeped into her lungs, adding a heaviness that seemed to drag at her chest. Cassie felt as if she were drowning in his unique scent. With a soft sigh, she allowed herself to relax completely, sagging against his hard chest as his lips met hers.

She'd been right, she thought distractedly. This was going to be a memorable vacation. *Very* memorable.

# Five

___

*"**P**sst!"*

Dan jumped as the discordant sound startled him. Curious, he looked around the empty hallway outside his bedroom door. Was Cassie's ghost having another try at frightening him?

*"Psst!"* The impatient hiss grew louder. "Over here."

Dan glanced down the hall in the direction of the sound and then wished he hadn't when he discovered an eye staring at him from a partially open door. Justin Sloan, he thought in resignation. He'd know that perfect blue orb anywhere.

He'd managed to avoid having to talk to Justin yesterday by staying close to Cassie, a situation that was beginning to appeal more and more to him. She was the most intellectually complex, sexually intriguing woman he'd ever met.

"Hurry up!" Justin beckoned him. "Someone might come."

"I live in hope," Dan muttered under his breath as he slipped into Justin's room.

Justin hurriedly closed the door behind him. "I didn't think I'd ever get a chance to talk to you alone," he complained.

"So talk." Dan made an effort to suppress his annoyance. Justin didn't want to be at China View any more than Dan wanted him here. Probably less.

"Harry is really worried," Justin related.

Dan shrugged, unimpressed. "Harry is always worried. He was born that way, and he'll probably get up out of his coffin at his funeral to make sure everything is going according to plan."

Justin studied him curiously. "Doesn't it bother you at all that Buczek is trying to have you killed?"

Dan twitched aside the sheer white curtains that covered the window and squinted down at the beach. He couldn't see anyone outside. Cassie must be busy with the details of running the inn this morning.

"You seem so blasé about the whole thing." Justin sounded as if he didn't know whether to admire his attitude or not.

Dan turned from the window. "A lot of people have tried to kill me over the years. No one can maintain panic stations for long periods of time. After a while you just start to get bored with the whole thing."

"Bored?" Justin sounded shocked. "How can you talk about boredom? Why, you've done more and seen more..." He sputtered to a stop.

Yeah, he'd seen more all right, Dan thought grimly. And a good deal of it replayed itself in his nightmares.

"Haven't you ever considered going into the broadcasting end of the business?" Justin asked enviously. "With your background and contacts, you wouldn't have any trouble at all getting an offer."

"I'm a reporter, not an actor. What did you want to see me about?" Dan tried to bring him to the point. "I thought we were supposed to pretend not to know each other so that you could keep an eye on things from a distance."

"There's not much to keep an eye on," Justin complained. "You and I are the only people here. Although that woman who checked me in might be worth getting to know. It's a good thing I had the foresight to plan ahead." Justin picked up a small silver packet from the top of the bureau and began to toss it from one hand to the other.

Dan felt a flash of raw anger as he recognized the package for what it was. He instinctively snatched it out of the air. "Stay away from her!" His harsh command echoed in the small room, surprising him as much as it did Justin. But even though he hadn't consciously meant to give it, Dan refused to retract the order. He didn't want Justin pestering Cassie. He shoved the package into his pocket, refusing to delve any further into the reason for his uncharacteristic possessiveness.

Justin raised his hands placatingly. "Hey, no problem. I didn't realize I was poaching. I just thought she might help to pass a boring few days."

Dan shrugged. "Sorry. I tried to tell Harry not to send you, that he was overreacting. But you know Harry."

"He may be right to worry this time. I promised him I'd guard you, and dammit, I will!" Justin's handsome features hardened, and for a moment he looked like someone else. Someone far more dangerous and, Dan conceded, far more interesting.

"Relax," he said soothingly. "I promise not to wander down any dark alleys. In exchange, you can satisfy my curiosity about something. Why did you choose the name of Smith?"

Justin gave him a smug smile. "Because Smith is so clichéd as an alias that no one would believe anyone would ever use it. So I did."

Dan blinked. There was a certain amount of logic to that. Not much common sense, but a certain amount of logic. His curiosity satisfied, he began to edge toward the door.

"Where are you going?" Justin looked at the notepad Dan was carrying.

"Downstairs. See you later." He escaped before Justin could think up an excuse to detain him.

Dan hurried down the steep front steps, barely noticing the twinges of his injured leg in his eagerness to find Cassie. At first he thought the lobby was deserted, but then he heard a muttered exclamation of annoyance from behind the reception desk. Silently, he leaned over the counter and peered down.

His heart rate accelerated when he saw the top of Cassie's head. He stared, fascinated at the way the late-morning sunlight splintered off the reddish strands of her hair. She'd yanked it back and fastened it with a rubber band. But despite her efforts, a number of curls had escaped to provide a sensual frame for her face. Bemused, he watched as she rubbed her forefinger over her nose, leaving a smudge of dust in its wake. More dust had landed on the front of her green silk shirt near her left breast.

A surge of desire slammed through him, catching him off guard. He wanted to brush away the dust from her small breast. He wanted to take Cassie in his arms and kiss each and every one of those tumbled curls framing her face. He wanted to taste the faint beads of moisture he could see under her eyes. He wanted to run his lips over the thick brush of her eyelashes.

Dan took a deep, steadying breath, faintly disturbed at his intense reaction to her. There had been no conscious thought on his part and certainly no enticement on hers. It was as if his body had an agenda that his mind didn't know about.

But what harm was there in it? he asked himself. He wasn't some impressionable youth to be swept away on a tide of passion. Not that the idea didn't have its appeal, he thought ruefully. But even if he were to lose his head, he'd seen no sign that Cassie was similarly inclined.

He leaned farther over the counter in order to see what she was doing. She appeared to be sorting through the piles of papers stacked on the shelves and littering the floor.

At his movement Cassie looked up, and a quick gleam of some sudden emotion that he hoped was pleasure, but feared was simply surprise, lit her grayish blue eyes.

"Good morning," she said. "Do you need something?"

Yes, you, he was tempted to say, but he bit back the impulsive words and walked around the desk to join her. Deciding not to compete for space on the littered floor, he sat down on the counter.

"I need an opinion." He shifted slightly, pulling a pen out from under his injured hip.

Cassie grinned at him. "You've come to the right place. I have a myriad assortment of opinions, and they're all correct."

Dan chuckled. "Careful, your advertising background is showing."

"Insults will get you nowhere. Besides, advertising serves a very useful purpose. Who does your company use?" She slipped the question in in the hope of gaining a solid fact to add to the pitiful few she had about him.

Dan blinked uncomprehendingly. "What?"

"Your insurance company. Who has their advertising account?"

"I don't know, and what's more I don't care," he rushed on when she opened her mouth. "I'm on vacation from work. I want you to tell me what you think about the editorial I've been working on."

Cassie gave up. Either he didn't know or for some reason he didn't want to tell her. Or he didn't really work for an insurance company. Whichever it was, if she persisted he might just disappear back into his room, where he'd spent most of the morning. And she didn't want that.

She leaned back against the wall and stared up at him, prepared to lend some practical help. By the time he'd finished reading the first paragraph it was obvious that Dan didn't need her help. Or anyone else's, for that matter. She frowned. He was a master of the written word.

"You don't like it?" He'd noticed her expression.

"On the contrary. I don't think anyone in our office could have written anything that good, myself included."

"Thank you." Dan was inordinately pleased by her praise. A pleasure that dimmed as he noticed the growing suspicion on her face.

"Which makes me wonder how an insurance salesman got to be so good," she went on, continuing her line of thought.

Deciding the best defense in this case might really be a good offense, he launched a counterattack. "There's no reason to be an intellectual snob."

Cassie blinked. "Me? A snob? I am not!"

"Then what do you call it when you automatically assume that an insurance salesman can't write?"

"I didn't say that," Cassie insisted defensively. "But you must admit that when people are as good at writing as you are they..." She trailed away into silence, not sure exactly what she did mean. All she was certain of was that her gut instinct told her there was more to this than met the eye.

"They what? Make their living at writing? Like a lot of people, I wanted to write the great American novel when I was in college." He gave her part of the truth.

"So what happened?"

"Reality," he said dryly. "I like to eat, and being a writer is a very precarious existence. I was offered a job with a steady paycheck and..." He shrugged. "The great American novel went on hold."

Cassie got to her feet and absently dusted off her beige linen shorts. "Personally, I think you sold out too soon. That editorial is a masterpiece of motivation. I predict the voters will pass that bond issue in a landslide, but—"

To Dan's relief, the bell on the front door jangled, and Cassie turned to see who'd come in. He didn't want to lie to her, but even less did he want to tell her the truth. At least, the truth about what he really did for a living. Despite the fact that Dan was sure Buczek would never manage to trace him here to the inn, always provided he'd managed to hire a hit man, Cassie might decide that he was too dangerous a person to have around. Not only that, but people tended to react strangely to the knowledge that he was an internationally known, Pulitzer Prize-winning newspaperman. And he liked the way Cassie reacted to him now, he decided as he scooted off the counter.

Cassie watched as a couple in their mid-thirties, accompanied by a small boy of about six, approached the desk. Please be guests, she prayed silently.

"Is this China View Guest House?" the woman asked.

Cassie watched her thin nose twitch with eagerness and was reminded of a white mouse she'd once had. "Yes, it is. How may I help you?"

"Is it true?" the man demanded, glancing furtively around the lobby as if looking for spies.

Ah, the rumor mill was alive and working well, Cassie thought in satisfaction.

"Is what true?" she asked brightly.

"I heard it from my hairdresser just this morning, and she had it from her niece, who heard it from Wilma."

"Wilma?" Cassie blinked, drawing a blank on the name.

"The checkout lady at the grocery store. But she's not important," the man said.

"Not to me," Cassie agreed, "but since I don't know what she said..."

"That there had been a sighting of a ghost," the woman intoned in a hushed whisper.

"Oh, that." Cassie tried to sound both offhand and mysterious. "I will admit I saw someone on the stairs, but to claim that it was a ghost just because it seemed to fade into thin air..."

"There! You see?" The woman turned triumphantly to her husband. "I knew it. This place must be a hundred years old."

"A hundred and fifty," Cassie corrected. "And just because the man I saw disappear looked exactly like the description of the original builder of China View is no reason to assume that he was a ghost."

"How about the fact that his eyes glowed phosphorescent yellow and he vanished right before my eyes?" Dan threw in helpfully, thoroughly enjoying himself.

"Nonsense!" Cassie pressed her lips together to keep from giggling at Dan's expression. He looked so smugly pleased with himself. "I've told you and told you that I don't believe in ghosts."

"Kill 'em," a voice offered.

Cassie leaned over the counter and peered down at the small boy there, slightly taken aback at his bloodthirsty expression.

"I gots me a slingshot." He held up a wicked-looking weapon that seemed more than capable of decimating the inn's bird population.

"There, there, Brett." His mother smiled fondly at him. "I told you. Mama wants to *study* the ghost."

"Then I'll kill it," Brett insisted.

"Then you can kill it," his father agreed. "Tell me, miss, has anyone else been out to study the ghost?"

"Of course not. There's no such thing as ghosts. I only mentioned it in passing to a few people because I thought they'd be as amused as I was."

Dan shivered theatrically. "I found him far too realistic to be amusing."

The man rubbed his hands together gleefully. "I can't believe our luck, Margo. We're going to have this sighting to ourselves. If only we hadn't had to bring..." He glanced down at his son, who was stretching the elastic band on the slingshot in a manner that made Cassie very nervous.

Margo sighed. "I know, but you know that Mama has a bad heart, and after what happened last time..."

After *what* happened last time? Cassie wondered with a speculative glance at Brett.

"Do you have two connecting rooms?" Margo asked. "We really should keep him close."

"The closer the better, from the looks of it," Dan muttered under his breath.

Cassie shot him a quelling look. It wasn't necessary that she like her guests, merely that they pay their bills. And from the looks of the gold credit card the man was handing her, that would not be a problem.

"Do you baby-sit?" Margo gave Cassie a hopeful look.

"Under no circumstances. And about that slingshot..."

"Oh, he wouldn't actually use it," Margo assured her with a perfectly straight face. "Our therapist says that if we allow Brett to vocalize his aggressions, then he won't be tempted to act them out."

Cassie opened her mouth, thought better of what she'd been about to say and finally said, "Speech is free, but if he breaks anything, it costs."

"Of course." The man signed the charge slip and accepted the keys Cassie handed him. "I'm Byron Essel, this is my wife, Margo, and I'm sure Brett won't be a problem."

"I'm Cassie Whitney, and this is Dan Travis," she said, keeping a cautious eye on Brett. She didn't trust the petulant thrust of his lower lip. Heaven only knew what he might do if he were to become bored. And there wasn't all that much to amuse a child around here.

"Tell me," Margo whispered with a furtive glance around the lobby. "What time does the ghost appear?"

"I saw him in the early evening," Dan related in a hoarse whisper. "He seemed to be floating in the air, and when I went to look closer, he disappeared."

Margo nodded happily. "That makes sense. According to our research, most sightings are either at dusk or dawn. Was that when you saw him, Miss Whitney?"

Cassie blinked. The last time she'd seen Jonas had been shortly after ten this morning. He'd been sitting in the kitchen in brilliant sunlight, wolfing down the molasses cookies she'd made earlier. There was nothing ethereal about Jonas. Of course, he wasn't a ghost, either, she conceded fairly.

"Dusk," she finally said, in the hopes that they would concentrate their search in the evenings. She didn't want them disturbing the other guests at the crack of dawn.

"Margo, our luck has changed," Byron chortled. "This will finally give our research the recognition it deserves."

"Yes, dear," Margo happily agreed as she trailed after her husband toward the stairs. "Come along, Brett." She threw the words over her shoulder.

To Cassie's relief, Brett, with one last speculative look at the huge Boston fern hanging in the side window, went.

"I sincerely hope that you intend to warn poor Jonas about that kid," Dan said.

"Ghosts don't need warnings," Cassie said, planning on doing exactly that.

Dan snorted. "That I know, but what does that have to do with warning Jonas?"

"If you want to be helpful, you could think of ways and means of separating that kid from his slingshot," Cassie suggested, ignoring the innuendo.

Dan leaned toward her. The warmth from his body seemed to flow around her, enclosing them in a small island of privacy. "What's it worth to you?" he whispered.

Cassie stared up into his eyes and felt a heaviness dragging at her stomach. She licked her lips, feeling a flash of excitement at the way his eyes narrowly followed her tongue's movement.

"What do you want?" she murmured, swaying toward him. Her breasts brushed against the rough cotton of his sweater and a shivery sensation shot through her.

"What are you two doing?" Brett's voice was like a shower of ice water.

"Didn't your mother ever tell you not to ask personal questions?" Dan's voice had a distinct edge to it.

"No," Brett said. "Were you going to kiss her?"

"I had something in my eye, and he was trying to see what it was," Cassie improvised.

Brett gave her a disgusted look that told her what he thought of that piece of fabrication. "I know all about kissing," he said in a superior tone that made Cassie want to laugh. "I go to a very progressive school."

Dan looked down at him for a long moment and then turned to Cassie. "I think I need to make a few additions to my editorial. There appears to be more to education than first meets the eye."

"It isn't the eyes meeting that's the problem," Cassie murmured sotto voce.

Dan gave her a look of mock astonishment. "No! Do tell. On second thought, you'd better not."

"Do you want something to eat?" she asked the boy. "I made some molasses cookies this morning."

"I want a soda. A real big soda," he demanded. "And a couple of candy bars. Put 'em on my dad's bill."

"Don't worry. I will," Cassie assured him.

"Say, lady, if somebody's dead and you kill 'em, are they dead a second time?"

"Sounds like a clear case of double jeopardy to me," Dan said. "But you might make the ghost mad, and since you can't kill him . . ." He allowed his voice to trail off suggestively.

"Hmm." Brett looked worried for a moment, then he brightened. "My mom wouldn't like it if the ghost was to waste me."

"Come to that, I wouldn't like it, either," Cassie said dryly. "Mangled bodies are very bad for business. But I might point out that there is a lot of ground between killing someone and all the little ways a ghost can get even. Now, you go into the sun-room, and I'll bring you your sugar snack," she ordered, hoping for Jonas' sake that Brett would take her warning to heart.

"I wonder if ghosts carry major medical." Dan's comment echoed Cassie's worries. "My personal opinion is that we ought to waylay the kid behind the potted plants and take away his chosen instrument of torture."

Cassie sighed. "Tempting, but we'd probably run afoul of the child-abuse laws."

Dan snorted. "Who's going to report us? His idiot parents? A kid deserves better than them. Even Brett."

Cassie eyed him as an image of a small boy with Dan's brown hair and eyes formed in her mind. A gleeful smile curved the childish lips and pure devilment danced in his eyes. An unconscious smile tugged at her own lips. She didn't doubt for a moment that Dan's child would be every bit as much a handful as Brett.

"Do you have any children?" Cassie winced when she heard herself ask the inane question. It was as bad as asking every man you met if he were married.

"No," he answered promptly. "Do you?"

"Of course not!" Cassie was annoyed at his question even though she was perfectly willing to admit that if it was acceptable for her to ask, it was also acceptable for him. "I am an innkeeper," she said, hoping to change the subject.

"No, your aunt is the innkeeper. Not that you'd know it." Dan looked around the empty lobby. "Where is she?"

"In Levington, organizing a rally to protest against some developer who wants to tear down one of the town's few apartment houses."

Dan grimaced. "So you have serpents here in paradise, too. Let me know if she has any success. I have a few New York developers I'd like to sic her on."

"Where's my candy?" Brett's voice echoed from the sunroom.

"Go get the brat his candy," Dan said. "Then I'll help you sort through all this . . ." He gestured toward the stacks of dusty material on the floor behind the counter.

"Stuff," Cassie supplied. "My aunt is a great collector of stuff. I'll be right back." She hurried out to the kitchen. The sooner she took care of Brett, the sooner she could get back to doing what she wanted to do—spend time with Dan. And although she would prefer to do it where they could be by themselves, behind the front desk was better than nothing.

She gave Brett an assortment of candy bars and a two-liter bottle of soda and then went back to the lobby.

She found Dan sitting on the floor behind the reception desk.

"Do you think your aunt would mind if I took these old newspapers I found under here?" He tossed them up on top of the counter.

Cassie waved a slender hand in the air to fan away the dust. "I doubt she'd even notice they're gone." She sat down on the floor beside him and reached past him to pull another stack off the shelf.

"I envy you this place," he said slowly. "Everyone in Levington seems to know everyone else. You must feel as if you belong." His voice was wistful, and Cassie studied him curiously.

"Did you grow up in New York City?" she asked.

"No. On a dairy farm in Wisconsin. I couldn't wait to get away from the smell of manure. I won a scholarship to Columbia and never went back. My mother died my sophomore year, and my father seemed to just kind of fade away without her. He died two years later. I sold the farm and that was that.''

No, Cassie thought, that wasn't that. There was a lot of unresolved pain in his stark recital of facts. Dan had never had a chance to get to know his parents as people in their own right. He'd gone directly from the normal teenage rebellion against their dominating role in his life to not having them at all. No wonder he felt something missing. A feeling that showed itself in envy of a small town where everything seemed simpler.

Cassie studied the tightly bracketed lines around his mouth, again wanting to comfort him. She wasn't even sure what she wanted to comfort him about. For the loss of his parents? That had happened long, long ago. For living in New York City instead of a small town? So did she, and she didn't feel it merited sympathy.

Unconsciously, she leaned toward him, intending to kiss his cheek. But at her movement, he turned toward her and her lips brushed against the side of his mouth. The beguiling texture of his freshly shaven skin sent a tingle of awareness through her, scattering her half-formed thoughts.

Enthralled by the feel of his lips, she slowly moved her head from side to side, savoring the sensation. Pleasure seeped through her mind, painting her thoughts with erotic fantasies.

"You are one very exciting woman, Cassie Whitney." Dan's husky voice added to her growing excitement. Her breath caught as his hand grasped the back of her neck, pulling her closer. His lips covered hers with a hunger he made no effort to disguise, and the tip of his tongue brushed against her lips.

Cassie shuddered. Dan made her feel like a teenager again, as if she were just discovering what love and life were all about. And she wasn't sure she liked the idea. Teenagers were very vulnerable. The disquieting thought surfaced through the pleasure swirling within her. Her confused thoughts were interrupted by the jingle of the bell as the front door opened.

Cassie drew back slightly. Her eyes were on a level with Dan's face, and as she watched, he opened his eyes and stared blankly at her as if he had found the kiss as disconcerting as she had.

Infinitesimal flecks of gold danced deep in his eyes and she gazed at them, wondering if those golden flecks would become even more noticeable if Dan and she were to make love.

"Is anyone here?" a shrill voice demanded.

Cassie tilted her head back and peered up. From her seat on the floor, all she could see was the ceiling. Whoever had come in was hidden from view. As she and Dan were, she realized thankfully.

Cassie glanced at Dan, who was watching her with a smoldering intensity that made her long to ignore the voice above them and snuggle back into his arms. She wanted to forget about the inn and all her responsibilities and just enjoy what the fates had been kind enough to send her way.

She stifled a sigh, her lower lip unconsciously dropping. She couldn't do that. Her aunt depended on her. And that voice might well want the last empty room.

Dan grimaced, his frustrated expression closely mirroring her own and gestured upward with his thumb.

Cassie nodded and, grabbing one of the stacks of papers to provide an excuse for having been lurking on the floor, got to her feet.

"Eck!" A middle-aged woman jumped back in alarm as Cassie suddenly appeared in front of her. "My goodness!" The woman placed a pudgy hand on her ample bosom. "How you startled me."

"Sorry," Cassie apologized. "I was simply cleaning out the shelves and didn't realize anyone was here at first. I..."

Her voice trailed away as she felt warm fingers lightly rubbing over the bare skin of her ankle. She licked her dry lips and edged away from the insidious stroking. It didn't work. Dan's caressing hand followed.

"One accumulates so much trash," Cassie said with a quelling stare downward.

"Oh, my yes," the woman agreed. "But then the minute you throw anything out, you find you need it."

Cassie suddenly tensed as Dan's caressing fingers wandered higher, to slowly stroke the sensitive skin behind her knee.

"How—" Her voice broke. She cleared her throat and went on. "How may I help you?"

"By telling me if it's true." The woman fixed beady black eyes on Cassie, her full lips pressed together in anticipation. "I just knew the minute that woman served the pumpkin pie—"

"The pie?" Cassie muttered distractedly, trying and failing to ignore Dan.

"At the restaurant where I stopped for lunch in that quaint little town of Levington. Or do you call them villages here? I'm from the Midwest myself and we just call them towns, but..." She paused. "Where was I?"

"The pie in the restaurant," Cassie murmured with a furtive glance down at Dan. He gave her an impossibly innocent look that made her long to smack him and kiss him at the same time. What was it about Dan Travis that seemed to bring so many different emotions to the fore, and in such a short time, too? she wondered uneasily.

"Oh, yes." The woman took a deep breath and rushed on, rather like a train roaring downhill. "The waitress in the restaurant was talking to another customer and she said that there had been a sighting here at this very inn. She gave me directions," the woman concluded triumphantly. "It is true, isn't it? I have so longed to make contact with the other world. You do have a ghost here, don't you?"

"We certainly have some very strange individuals in residence." Cassie shook her leg free of Dan's fingers, which were now drawing erotic patterns on her skin. "But as for ghosts, I personally don't believe in them. Something was seen, but I'm sure that there is a perfectly reasonable explanation for it," she said, reciting her stock piece.

The woman clasped her hands together theatrically. "The explanation is fate. The fates have rewarded me for a lifetime of searching by making sure that I was here when this sighting was made. This will be the culmination of my lifetime's work."

"Oh?" Cassie eyed her uneasily.

The woman drew herself up proudly and announced, "I, my dear, am Madam Rowinski."

"Ah, I see," Cassie murmured, seeing nothing of the sort. "That would explain it."

"I am a medium of no small repute," Madam Rowinski continued. "Why, back home in Illinois, the police are always asking for my help in solving the most baffling of crimes."

Cassie's stomach twisted as Dan's wandering fingers inched up along her inner thigh.

Madam Rowinski nodded in satisfaction. "I don't doubt you are astonished. I have an enviable reputation. And now to be able to study a real, live ghost..."

Cassie opened her mouth to point out that *real, live* and *ghost* were not compatible terms and then thought better of it. Logic did not appear to be Madam Rowinski's strong suit. Not that it mattered. As long as the woman could pay for her room, she could be as inconsistent as she wanted.

Although Cassie would have to warn Jonas. Poor man, she thought, feeling a prickle of guilt. She'd have to give him a bonus. Between Brett and the threat of his slingshot and Madam Rowinski, who would probably talk him to death, he deserved something more tangible than sympathy.

"You do have a room, don't you?" Madam Rowinski leaned forward in sudden agitation. "Please, tell me you have a small corner I can inhabit. Otherwise I'll have to sleep in the car while I search for the ghost."

"That won't be necessary." Cassie cut off the seemingly inexhaustible flow of words. "We have one room left."

"Ah." Madam Rowinski gave her a beaming smile. "You see, I was right. The fates have indeed blessed me today." She signed the register Cassie hurriedly pushed toward her.

"How long will you be staying with us and how will you be paying for the room?" Cassie asked.

Madam Rowinski pressed her lips together thoughtfully. "Three days, maybe longer, and I'll pay..." She rummaged through her oversize, black vinyl purse. Extracting several hundred-dollar bills, she handed them to Cassie. "I don't believe in credit cards," she confided. "Nasty things, always tempting you to spend more than you can afford."

Of course she didn't believe in credit cards, Cassie thought ruefully. With the exception of the Essels, no one around this place seemed to. Cassie dropped the bills into the strongbox, handed Madam Rowinski the key and directed her to her room.

"Is it safe to come up yet?" Dan hissed.

Cassie watched Madam Rowinski disappear up the stairs and then said, "Yes, she's out of sight."

"Which is what I'd best be." Dan glanced at his watch and his earlier expression of teasing indulgence fled. "I promised to talk to Ed this afternoon, and I'm going to be late." He grabbed his editorial off the counter and, with a warm smile at Cassie, rushed out.

Talk to Ed about what? Cassie wondered. The editorial? Insurance? Maybe Ed just wanted to talk to Dan because Dan was an interesting person. She certainly did. But then she very much doubted that Ed's interest was quite the same as hers, she thought ruefully.

# Six

"**O**h, there you are, dear." Hannah stuck her head into the tiny room off the lobby that served as an office. "I wanted to ask you if you knew just how closely a judge looks at the signatures on a petition."

Cassie looked up from the inn's books, which she'd been working on since breakfast, studied her aunt's worried expression for a moment and then asked, "Why?"

"Well, I very much fear that Jessie, in her enthusiasm to stop the developer, has convinced herself that the ends justify the means."

"And I take it they don't?"

"Not when the names she signed to the petition came from the tombstones in the cemetery." Hannah sighed. "Someone's bound to notice. They always do when you don't want them to."

Cassie chuckled. "It would appear that we aren't the only ones making use of the dearly departed. Although we seem to be having better success." She gestured toward the account books with satisfaction.

"Being full does give one such a feeling of security, doesn't it?" Hannah's expression brightened momentarily. "But I really should go into town and see what I can do to repair the damage Jessie's impetuosity has caused. What are your plans for the day, dear?"

Find Dan. The appealing thought popped into her mind. It seemed so long since she'd seen him yesterday. His visit to Ed's must have run very late because, despite the fact that she'd sat in the lounge until after eleven trying to give the impression that she was casually reading, he still hadn't returned when she'd finally given up and gone to bed. She had too much pride to allow a man, even one as fascinating as Dan Travis, to think she had nothing better to do with her time than sit around waiting for him to put in an appearance.

"I'm not sure what I plan to do once I finish with the books," Cassie hedged.

"Well, if you should decide to go out, just ask Gertie to keep an eye on things. She's upstairs cleaning the bedrooms."

"Have you seen Jonas this morning?" Cassie asked. "I have his pay for him."

"He's in the kitchen sampling the chocolate-chip cookies I made this morning."

Cassie chuckled. "Of course he's eating. What I can't figure out is why he doesn't weigh three hundred pounds."

"I like a man who appreciates his food," Hannah insisted. "Not like that Mr. Smith, who kept asking me what the saturated-fat content of all the breakfast dishes were."

"Don't worry about him. One more scare like Jonas gave him last night and our Mr. Smith will be hightailing it back to wherever it was he came from."

"It can't be any too soon as far as I'm concerned." Hannah settled her old felt hat more firmly on her head. "If you should need me, I'll be at Jessie's. Unless, of course, I succumb to the temptation to strangle her. Then I'll be at the police station."

Cassie laughed at her aunt's bellicose expression. "If you do, be sure you hire her as a ghost. We'd have a matched set."

Hannah merely shook her head in disgust as she left.

Cassie stashed the account books in the desk drawer, and picking up the envelope that contained Jonas' pay, went to give it to him.

She found him in the kitchen.

"Good morning, Jonas. Here's your money." She set the envelope down on the table beside him. "And I wanted to compliment you on your haunting of Mr. Smith last night."

"Nothing to it. He's an easy one to spook because he thinks he knows it all."

Cassie grimaced. "He does rather give the impression of being above us lesser mortals, doesn't he? I don't like him. What's more, I don't trust him."

"Bah! No need to worry about him. Ran across his like before. He'd never do anything to dirty his clothes. Strange, though, he doesn't seem like the type China View would appeal to." Jonas absently brushed cookie crumbs off his beard. "And he didn't come to see a ghost, either. Not like the rest of those caper-witted idiots who showed up yesterday."

"Madam Rowinski isn't too bad. Why don't you give her a small fright? We don't want her to feel left out."

"Rather not." Jonas frowned, the thick black bar of his eyebrows almost meeting over the bridge of his large nose. "Don't like her aura," he muttered.

"Her aura?" Cassie stared at him in surprise. "Jonas, don't you dare start getting temperamental on me. I have enough problems."

"Don't like her aura," Jonas repeated stubbornly. "Can I have some of these cookies to take with me?"

"Sure. Help yourself. Jonas, have you seen any of our guests this morning?" She tried to make the question sound casual.

Jonas wasn't fooled. "You mean like that nice lad who's sweet on you?"

"He isn't sweet on me?" Cassie was unable to prevent the question that crept into her voice.

"He always looks for you when he comes into a room. Not only that, but his eyes kind of light up when he finds you. We called that being sweet on a gal when I was young."

"We still do, if it's true." Cassie tried to sound matter-of-fact, when what she wanted was to pump Jonas for more information. But he could be saying that because he thought it was what she wanted to hear. A frisson of doubt crept into her mind. Jonas *was* basically a very kind man.

She watched him studying the plateful of cookies as he tried to decide which to eat next. Did she really want to hear that Dan was sweet on her?

Yes, she finally concluded. And she wanted to hear it because *she* was sweet on *him*. She found Dan Travis fascinating, both physically and mentally. And somehow the possibility that her feelings might be reciprocated seemed to intensity them.

Cassie glanced up at the clock, rather surprised to find that it was almost noon. She'd spent the entire morning bringing the inn's books up-to-date and now she was entitled to enjoy herself, she thought as she left Jonas to his cookies and went to find Dan. She hoped he hadn't already left the inn.

She looked out the lobby window at the guests' parking area. Dan had to be around somewhere, she realized with a rising sense of anticipation when she saw his car still parked next to Smith's. Perhaps he'd gone for a walk along the shore? She turned and started toward the sun-room, which had the best view of the beach.

"Ah, there you are, Miss Whitney." Margo called down to her from the top of the stairs.

Cassie pinned a polite smile on her face and, reigning in her impatience, said, "Good morning, Mrs. Essel. Did you need something?"

"I don't suppose you'd be willing to make an exception and baby-sit for Brett today, would you?"

"Sorry," Cassie lied.

"I didn't think you would." Margo sighed. "We'll just have to take him with us. Since ghosts never appear during the daylight hours, we're going to drive up the coast and see if we can't find some wild tansy."

"Tansy?"

"It draws spirits," Margo said earnestly. "And since that selfish Mr. Smith wouldn't tell us anything about his experience last night..." She clicked her tongue in annoyance. "It just doesn't seem fair that the ghost would choose to manifest itself to a nonbeliever like Mr. Smith when we were waiting for him."

It would if Brett was part of the reception committee, Cassie thought dryly. "Perhaps the tansy will work," she said soothingly.

"Oh, I hope so. We absolutely must have a picture of him to add weight to the sighting."

And to expose the impersonation, Cassie realized, making a mental note to warn Jonas that the Essels had a camera with them.

"But we will definitely be back in time for supper." Margo gave Cassie a distracted smile and disappeared back up the stairs.

Tansy! Cassie shook her head at the gullibility of some people.

"Good morning, Miss Whitney." Madam Rowinski greeted her as she entered the sun-room. "Beautiful morning, isn't it?"

"Yes." Cassie used Madam Rowinski's observation as an excuse to stick her head out the French doors and look toward the beach. Her heartbeat accelerated as she caught sight of Dan down at the shoreline. He was talking to Justin Smith.

It was odd, Cassie mused. Smith was wearing a skimpy pair of running shorts that were plastered to his perfectly sculpted, sweat-dampened body and yet she felt absolutely no interest in him at all. But Dan . . .

Her breath caught in her throat as she watched the way the brisk wind off the ocean molded his khaki slacks to his taut thighs. She only had to see him and she wanted to touch him. To explore every inch of his beguiling body.

Her absorption was abruptly shattered when Smith suddenly leaned toward Dan, his whole attitude one of aggression. Or anger. Cassie heard the sharp tone of Smith's voice, but she couldn't quite make out his words.

Curious, she looked at Dan. He seemed more bored than annoyed by whatever it was that Smith was saying. Cassie watched as Smith turned and gestured emphatically toward the inn. Dan merely shrugged.

They didn't argue like recent acquaintances, Cassie thought uneasily. They argued as if they knew each other— and didn't much like what they knew. But if they knew each other, then why pretend not to? Why would either of them care what anyone at China View thought?

Madam Rowinski twitched aside the filmy white curtains and looked out to see what Cassie found so interesting. "Ah, if only I were thirty years younger. That Mr. Smith is quite a dish, isn't he?"

"Almost too good to be true," Cassie muttered, watching as Smith brought his hand down in a chopping, negative gesture and stalked toward the house, leaving Dan staring after him.

"How strange," Madam Rowinski murmured. "Kind of makes you wonder what got Mr. Smith's dander up."

It sure does, Cassie thought. Not that she was likely to find out. Questioning Dan had to be the ultimate exercise in futility.

"Poor Mr. Travis." Madam Rowinski clicked her tongue in sympathy. "He looks kind of lost standing there all by himself, doesn't he?"

No, not really. Cassie mentally refuted the idea. He looked . . . regal. In total command of both himself and the elements. Mesmerized, she watched as the wind blew through his hair, lifting each individual strand. Her skin tingled with the compulsive urge to follow suit, to run her fingers through his hair. To savor the texture of it. To smell the sun-tanged aroma of his skin. To—

"You ought to take a thermos of coffee and a snack and go have a picnic on the beach with Mr. Travis," Madam Rowinski suggested. "I sure would if I were a few years younger."

"It *is* a nice day," Cassie murmured as she considered the idea. It would be fun to sit on the beach and eat sandwiches, drink coffee and... A hectic flush burned across her skin. The "and" part in particular appealed to her. But would it be wise to allow what she already felt for Dan to deepen? she wondered. To allow herself the luxury of expressing her fascination with him on a physical level? She didn't really know that much about Dan Travis.

And most of what she did know wasn't factual knowledge, but based on gut feeling. It was her instinctive, elemental reaction to him, and just how reliable was that reaction? She didn't know. But it wasn't as if she were some starry-eyed teenager expecting love and happily-ever-after endings, she rationalized. An unexpected sense of loss pressed down on her. Dan Travis didn't give off happy-ever-after vibes. But that didn't mean she couldn't enjoy his company while he was here, she told herself as she watched him head down the beach, his movements slow as if his leg were bothering him.

"Go on. Go after him," Madam Rowinski urged.

"I think I will take a snack and follow him." Cassie found the temptation irresistible. "If you'll excuse me, I have to let Gertie know that I'm going out."

"Good luck with your hunting." Madam Rowinski picked up her knitting.

Cassie gave her a wry look, but refrained from commenting. Instead, she hurried up the front stairs, ran Gertie to ground in Smith's room and told her where she was going. The fact seemed to elicit no interest from Gertie whatsoever. She was far too busy grumbling about the mess Smith had left his bathroom in and that she knew his kind never left a tip.

But what was Smith's kind? Cassie wondered as she hurried down the back stairs. His kind certainly came with money. If the quality of his clothes hadn't already told her, then a quick glance at the line of expensive male cosmetics lining his bureau would have. He either had independent means or a very well paid job.

She gasped in horrified outrage as she walked into the kitchen and discovered Brett carving the edge of the antique maple table with a twelve-inch butcher knife. A razor-sharp, twelve-inch butcher knife.

"Put that down!" she ordered, fear making her voice harsh.

The boy turned and gave her a bored look. "I was just seeing how sharp it was."

"Nowhere near as sharp as my temper! Put it down."

"Aw, nobody ever lets me have any fun," he whined. "I was just looking for that ghost that frightened that man in the room next to us last night."

To Cassie's relief, Brett did let go of the knife. She hurriedly grabbed it and shoved it onto the top shelf of the cabinets, hopefully out of his reach. She would have to warn her aunt to hide the knives until Brett and his family left.

"Out," she ordered. "And under no circumstances are you to come back in here, understand?"

"I'm going to tell my mother on you!" Brett threatened loudly.

"You won't have to tell her," Cassie said. "I'll tell her myself. Now out!"

Brett left, grumbling as he went.

Cassie shut the door behind him and then hurried to fix a quick snack before Dan got too far down the beach and she couldn't find him. She threw together two roast-beef sandwiches and filled a thermos with coffee, adding cream and sugar with a liberal hand in the hopes of disguising the fact that it was left over from breakfast.

She was packing the food into a picnic basket when she noticed that the envelope she'd given Jonas earlier was still on the table.

She checked inside, thinking he might have taken out the money, but he hadn't. It was all still there.

Cassie frowned at the painted tin milk pitcher full of dried flowers on the windowsill. Why hadn't Jonas taken it? Surely he needed the money? Why else would he be working for minimum wage? She glanced over at the plate of cookies. It was empty, and a reluctant smile curved her lips. One thing was certain. He didn't need the money to buy food. He ate plenty here.

She set the envelope beside the flowers. He'd probably heard Brett coming and had hastily flitted out the back-door. And characteristically, when he'd reached for something to save, it had been the food, she thought ruefully.

Cassie grabbed the picnic basket and stepped outside. As she'd expected, Dan was already out of sight, so she started in the direction he'd been going.

She trudged through the loose sand, heading for the shoreline where the sand was more closely packed. Ignoring the gulls that screamed angrily at her intrusion into what they obviously considered their private domain, Cassie shaded her eyes against the bright sunlight and squinted into the distance. A sense of exhilaration gripped her as she caught sight of a solitary figure farther up the beach. It had to be Dan. Her pace automatically quickened.

She broke into a trot when Dan caught sight of her and paused to wait.

"Hi," she panted as she caught up with him. "I saw you out for a walk and, since I was ready for a break, I packed a snack and came along."

Dan's lips lifted in a slow smile that sent a surge of warmth through her. Cassie felt her own lips move upward in an involuntary response. Her attention was caught by the glint in his bright eyes. He really was glad to see her. His welcome was clear in his face—a welcome he made no attempt to hide. Cassie felt a strange sense of power envelope her. When he smiled at her like that, she felt capable of anything.

Dan took the basket and caught her hand in his. His fingers curled possessively around hers, but his grasp didn't make her feel trapped. It made her feel safe. Safe, protected and wanted. She ran the tip of her tongue over her dry lips and shot him a quick glance, to find him watching her with absorbed interest. Suddenly, the day seemed brighter and in much sharper focus.

"There's a place farther down the beach that will be perfect for a private picnic," he said. "I found it on my walk yesterday."

Cassie fell into step beside him.

Five minutes later Dan waved an expansive hand toward a secluded cove that was tucked between a rocky outcrop and a sand dune. "My discovery," he announced.

Cassie chuckled at his pleased expression. "Sorry, Columbus, we used to play here when I was a kid because the rocks hid us from any adult who wanted to find us." She glanced up and down the beach. Her sense of anticipation skyrocketed when she realized that, as usual, it was deserted.

She moved back from the shoreline and, sitting down on some thick tufts of dune grass, unpacked her basket.

Dan picked up a cookie and began to munch it. "Delicious," he pronounced. "Your aunt could give cooking lessons."

"Mrs. Veach is a pretty fair cook herself," Cassie hinted, wondering if Ed had taken him home to dinner and that was what had kept him out so late.

Dan grimaced. "You couldn't prove it by me. Ed's press broke down, and we had to wait until after eleven for someone to arrive from Portsmouth to fix it. We wound up sending out for hamburgers." He absently picked up another cookie. "That equipment is in very bad shape. This can't be the first deadline Ed's missed."

Cassie shrugged. "I wouldn't know. I'm not here often enough to keep that close a watch on local happenings. Ask Aunt Hannah. She knows everything. Although even Aunt Hannah can't seem to get a handle on your Mr. Smith." Cassie redirected the conversation with more purpose than finesse.

"He isn't my Mr. Smith. How about one of those sandwiches? I don't know what it is about the sea air, but it gives me an appetite."

"And I don't know what it is about Smith that sends you retreating into platitudes," Cassie said tartly, handing him one of the sandwiches.

"I simply find him a boring subject."

"And I find him a worrisome subject. If he's as harmless as you say, why does he trail along after you? He left the inn yesterday shortly after you did."

"Did he?" Dan seemed unperturbed at the news. "He didn't show up at the newspaper office."

"And he searched your room the minute he arrived here," she persisted.

"But I'll bet he didn't get half as much information as that cleaning lady of yours," Dan said wryly. "I found her going through my drawers."

"She was probably just straightening them." Cassie defended the inquisitive Gertie. "At least she's harmless. She doesn't argue with you like Smith was this morning."

"Oh, arguing is a rather strong way to put it."

"Then how would you put it?"

"He was simply asking my opinion about something and didn't like my answer."

Cassie pressed her lips together in frustration. It was obvious Dan wasn't going to tell her anything. It was also obvious that he didn't think Smith was a problem. Why? Because Dan knew all about Smith and thus could dismiss him as a danger? But if he did know, why not tell her? Was it possible that Smith was a rival from another insurance company? But surely the insurance business wasn't all that cloak and dagger? If Dan really was in the insurance business, she thought uneasily, remembering her earlier doubts.

"What do you really do for a living?" she asked, watching as the skin on his cheekbones tightened. She was making him angry. But even knowing it, she couldn't drop the subject. It nagged at her. Her lack of any real, concrete knowledge about him and his past and, what was worse, his future, filled her with a sense of panic. And her panic seemed to grow in direct proportion to her burgeoning feelings for him.

"I told you. I sell insurance. How about some of that coffee?"

Cassie poured him a cup. "I know what you told me. But what I asked was what you did for a living?" She refused to back down.

"You're allowing your imagination to run away with you," Dan insisted. "First you're seeing ghosts, and now you're seeing... Exactly what is it you think you're seeing?" He gave her a condescending smile that absolutely infuriated her. All the more so because she was relatively certain he was doing it on purpose to try to shut her up.

She plunked the thermos down on the sand with a thud and jumped to her feet. Her sense of frustrated anger made her movements jerky.

"I refuse to sit here and allow you to patronize me!" she snapped.

"Cassie!" Dan reached for her. "I didn't mean... It's just that..."

"What? That I'm asking questions you have no intention of answering? All right. You can sit here and relish your privacy. I have better things to do." She stalked away.

"Cassie!" Dan awkwardly scrambled to his feet. "You don't understand."

"How can I when you won't explain it to me?" She threw the question over her shoulder.

"Cassie, be reasonable." Catching up with her at the edge of the dune, he grabbed her arm.

She jerked back in negation of the unwelcome feeling that flooded through her at his touch. Losing her balance, she fell to the sand. Dan, none too steady on his feet in the first place, was pulled off balance and fell on top of her.

"Get off of me, you overgrown oaf!" she muttered, trying to wiggle out from beneath him. All she accomplished was to make herself far more aware of him, of the collection of hard bone and lean muscle that comprised Dan Travis. Of the salt-scoured scent of his skin. Of the warmth of his flesh pushing her into the soft, dry sand at the base of the dune.

"Don't move!" he gasped. "My leg..."

Cassie froze, her anger evaporating beneath her concern. Fearfully, her eyes searched his face.

"Dan?" She cupped his cheek and agitatedly ran her palm over his jawline. "I'm sorry! I may have wanted to smack you, but I didn't mean to hurt you."

"That's some consolation at least." He let his breath out in a long, shaky sigh as he gingerly rolled off her onto his back, covering his eyes with his forearm.

Raising up on her knees, Cassie stared down at the deeply etched lines beside his mouth, very much fearing that pain from his wounded leg had carved them there. A wound caused by another bullet? Instinctively, her eyes swung down to his right leg. She was distracted by a silvery glitter in the sand near his hip.

Curious, she reached down and picked up the small, flat object. A sense of exhilaration welled within her as she recognized it. She hadn't misread Dan's interest in her. He *did* want to make love to her.

"Let me guess. You were a Boy Scout?"

Dan lifted has arm off his eyes and peered up at her. "Actually, I was. But what brought that on?"

"The fact that you appear to operate under the motto of Always Be Prepared." She held up the silver-foil packet.

Damn Justin! Dan thought in frustration when he realized the package must have come out of his pocket when they'd fallen. Now what should he say? He could hardly tell Cassie where he'd really gotten it. That would lead to telling her the truth about Justin Smith, which would inevitably lead to the truth about who he was and why the pair of them were hiding out at China View. And *that* bit of knowledge could quite possibly end his developing relationship with Cassie. At the very least, it might deal it a severe setback. It might take him the rest of his stay to recoup his position.

On the other hand, he didn't want Cassie to think he was the kind of man who always carried condoms so that he'd be free to indulge in quick sex with any chance-met women. He wanted her to know he didn't just want to have sex with her but wanted to make love to her. Make love to her with all the implications for a continuing relationship.

His eyes narrowed as he caught the gleam of laughter sparkling in her bright eyes. She didn't look angry at him for having it. She looked...amused, he finally decided. Perhaps his best bet would be to try a harmless lie that might appeal to her sense of humor.

"Actually," he said, "when I picked that up, I was thinking about your job."

Cassie blinked. "My job?"

"I was just wondering what kind of campaign a modern woman like you would design to sell condoms."

Cassie studied him speculatively. She didn't believe his explanation for one moment. On the other hand, she had to give him points for originality. And exploring his lie certainly held some intriguing possibilities. She felt a burgeoning sense of excitement.

"An ad campaign for condoms." She gave him a slow, seductive smile that slammed through him, releasing the breath he'd been holding.

"In a campaign like that, image is everything. I think I'd start with stills for the more-sophisticated magazines."

She rocked back on her heels and studied him through slitted eyes. "Since we're selling sex—"

"Relationships," he corrected, sitting up in the sand. "We're selling relationships."

"Relationships," Cassie repeated in satisfaction. She didn't know how much of what Dan was saying applied to the situation between them and how much was just banter, but at least he understood that there was a difference between sex and a relationship. A fact that distinguished him from ninety percent of the men she'd dated.

"What we want to project is the image of a man in control of himself and his surroundings." She grasped his chin in her fingers and turned his head to one side, as if studying his profile. In truth, she was busily savoring the texture of the tautly stretched skin of his jawline.

"A right profile, I think. Look out to sea as if you're searching the horizon," she ordered.

Dan obediently turned.

"No, not quite. You need to look a little more..." Cassie ran her fingers through his silky hair, creating a tousled look that made her think of abandoned kisses and long sensual nights.

"My neck is getting a crick," he complained.

"One must suffer for art's sake," Cassie loftily informed him. "Let me see." She cocked her head to one side and studied his perfect profile appreciatively. "No, we aren't quite there yet. We need to reinforce your basic sensuality. Take your sweater off," she ordered, her breath catching in her lungs as she waited to see what his reaction would be.

Dan seemed only too eager to cooperate. He yanked it off and carelessly tossed it behind him.

Fascinated, Cassie stared at the whorls of dark brown hair that covered his broad chest. Her fingers tingled with a compulsive urge to touch him. To discover the exact texture of that hair.

"Brace yourself on one elbow like this." Using the excuse of helping him pose, she grasped the supple skin of his shoulders and then leaned back, letting her fingers trail slowly down over his chest as she went. His crisp body hair scraped over her palms, and she shivered in reaction. She flexed her fingertips, pressing them into the smooth muscle layer of his broad chest.

Cassie watched the small golden flecks in Dan's eyes move in agitated circles, and the tension gripping her tightened its hold. The game she had instigated was fast becoming something else, something far more serious. Something she craved with an intensity that she might have found worrisome if she'd been in the mood to think.

"We aren't quite there yet." Her voice reflected her escalating tension.

Dan suddenly stood up, taking her by surprise. She leaned back and stared up at him. From her position at his feet he looked enormous.

"The problem," he said, "is that men don't make love with their pants on."

"Oh?" Mesmerized, Cassie watched as he unbuckled his belt and slowly, far too slowly, unzipped his slacks. He deftly shrugged out of them and his briefs and tossed them after his sweater. He turned and stared out to sea.

"Is this what you had in mind?" he asked.

Cassie gulped. Only in her wildest dreams, she thought, her eyes glued to the magnificent proportions of his body. There wasn't an ounce of superfluous fat anywhere on him. He looked like an artist's idealized portrait of masculinity. Her eyes dropped to his groin, and a burst of desire exploded in her, making her giddy. She swallowed longingly. She wanted to make love to him, and she wanted to do it now.

"Almost." She forced the word out past her dry throat.

"Almost? You know what the trouble is?"

Yes, I know exactly what the trouble is! Cassie thought in acute frustration. We're carrying on a conversation when what I really want to do is to kiss you, starting at your mouth and working my way down to— Her eyes dropped to his flagrant masculinity.

"The problem," he continued, seemingly unconcerned by either her wide-eyed stare or his own nakedness, "is that I don't know what my motivation is."

"Motivation?" she parroted.

"You know—what's my goal? What's motivating me? For example, wouldn't you say that a man who was thinking about needing a condom would naturally be thinking about making love to a beautiful woman?"

"Umm, I guess so," Cassie muttered, wondering how to regain control of a situation that seemed to be fast slipping away from her.

"Then we're agreed. I should be thinking about a beautiful woman," he continued. "And since I'm going to make love to her, she should be naked. Unfortunately, I can't bring to mind a beautiful, naked woman."

Cassie took a deep breath, ensnared by the glow burning deep in his eyes. "You suffer from short-term memory loss, do you?"

Dan grinned at her, and Cassie stared in fascination at his mouth. She wanted to kiss it and taste it and—

"So if you'd just take off your clothes..." he suggested in a perfectly normal tone of voice.

"My clothes?" Cassie dragged her eyes away from the shape of his mouth and concentrated on what his mouth was saying.

"To motivate me," he explained, with an innocence belied by the wicked gleam of laughter in his eyes.

Slowly Cassie got to her feet. She wanted to do just that, she conceded. She wanted to throw away every vestige of civilization and revel in the naturalness of what she was feeling. Surreptitiously, she glanced around, but they were effectively screened from view from anyone approaching along the shore, and the ocean was empty as far as the eye could see.

She took a deep breath and slowly slipped out of her blouse, tossing it on top of his sweater. The wonder on his face fed her sense of rightness at what she was doing and she hastily unfastened her bra and then slipped out of her shorts and panties, dropping them on top of her blouse.

Proudly, she straightened herself to her full height and asked, "Are you motivated yet?"

"Right out of my mind," he said hoarsely. Reverently he reached for her and gently, ever so gently, ran his fingertips from the center of her collarbone out to her shoulders and then down her chest to linger across her breasts.

Cassie gulped in the salty tang of the sea air overlaid with the faint musk of his cologne. The erotic combination seemed to intensify the sensations spreading from his wandering fingers.

"You're so beautiful," he muttered as he grasped her waist and pulled her down onto the sand, where he crouched beside her. "Once, when I was six, my grandfather gave me five dollars to spend. I remember standing in front of the candy store and looking at all the goodies, feeling the power it gave me to know that they were all within my grasp. I just had to decide where to start. I look at you and feel the exact same way," he said. "And I think I'll start . . ." He lowered his head and nuzzled the skin behind her ear with his firm lips.

Cassie gasped as he began to paint erotic patterns on her sensitized skin with the hot tip of his tongue. Blindly, she reached for him, her fingers threading through his wind-ruffled hair to curl tenaciously around his warm scalp. She wanted him and she was willing to admit it—to herself as well as to him. Whatever she did or didn't know about Dan Travis, she trusted her feelings about him. Demandingly, she tugged his head down. His open mouth met hers with blatant hunger, and her thoughts scattered like dry leaves before a brisk autumn wind.

His heavier body pressed her into the soft, shifting sand, and the gritty texture scraped her bare back, heightening her awareness of him. Dan pushed his tongue into her mouth with a possessiveness that thrilled her. Eddying ripples of tension skated over her nerves as slowly, painstakingly, he began to explore the velvety inside of her mouth. Her tension tightened, compacting her into a pulsating entity whose only desire was to feel. To relish how Dan was making her feel and then to ride the emotion to its inevitable conclusion.

Cassie engaged his tongue in a duel, and a feeling of omnipotence surged through her as she felt a shudder rack his body. She might not know everything she wanted to about him, but she did know he was as susceptible to her as she was to him.

He tore his mouth away from hers and stared down into her flushed face, an awed expression in his eyes. That expression fed Cassie's sense of feminine power. Not only did he want her, but he quite obviously valued her. She was a real person to him and not just an available woman.

Wonderingly, she traced a fingertip over his eyebrows and down the straight bridge of his nose, smiling inwardly as he shuddered again. "You are gorgeous," she said, and to her surprise his skin took on a faint reddish hue she found endearing.

He brushed the tips of his roughened knuckles over her taut breasts, and Cassie gasped as pinpricks of excitement shafted through her, seeming to collect in her abdomen. Her dusky pink nipples convulsed in an agony of longing and she waited, seemingly suspended in time, as he encircled her small breast with his hand. Heat poured from his fingers, and her breasts swelled in reaction. Cassie felt as if she'd been waiting her entire life for this moment and this man.

Dan lowered his head and the warmth of his breath drifted across her skin, tightening it unbearably. And then his mouth closed with greedy intensity over her nipple, suckling strongly.

A silvery shard of feeling pierced her breast, racing through her pliant flesh. The sensation seemed to swirl round and round, gathering force as it moved. She felt as if she were being inexorably pulled toward a conflagration the likes of which she could only imagine.

"Dan!" she gasped, clutching his shoulders and frantically rubbing her hands over his heated skin. "I want you."

"The feeling is entirely mutual," he muttered. As Cassie watched through narrowed eyes, he carefully positioned himself between her legs and leaned forward. The heat pouring from him wrapped protectively around her slight frame a moment before he penetrated her welcoming body.

Cassie felt reaction rip through her as she shifted to accommodate him. He was going too slow, she thought frantically. She wanted him to go faster. To intensify the forces building within her. Digging her heels into the sand, she levered herself upward, forcing him even deeper. For a brief, fantastic moment it was sufficient, and then suddenly it wasn't. She craved more. She needed to go farther down the road he'd set them on, and only Dan held the magical key to take them.

"Dan!" She gasped his name, excitement making it hard for her to articulate her needs.

"Slowly!" he begged her, his voice harsh and his face a rigid mask of concentration. "I can't... I'm not..."

"You're perfect," she responded without understanding what he was trying to say. "Absolutely—Dan!" Her keening sound of disbelief was swallowed up by his mouth as his lips covered hers. She felt as if her insides were being wound tighter and tighter, and then suddenly the tension snapped and she was hurling into an endless abyss of hot, swirling sensation that poured through her mind and permeated the farthest reaches of her body.

Just as she was starting to surface from the maelstrom, she felt Dan's muscles contract and then convulse as his own release overtook him and he collapsed onto her.

A small, secretive smile curved her lips as she ran her fingers along his sweat-dampened spinal column, pausing to lovingly explore each bump. She felt wonderful. Invigorated. As if nothing in the world could ever harm her again.

"I'm too heavy for you," he muttered as he rolled off her onto the grass-covered sand. With the loss of their closeness, her sense of omnipotence began to fade, allowing her doubts to creep in.

"Thank you," he murmured, his breath stirring the hair around her ear. "Thank you very much."

"You're welcome," Cassie replied inanely, when what she wanted to do was ask questions. Such as what had what they'd just shared really meant to him? What had he meant when he'd talked about establishing relationships? Did he mean that his feelings for her went deeper than merely a vacation romance, or was that wishful thinking on her part? She couldn't think of anyone to ask without sounding like a pathetically insecure woman. He'd made no promises to her, she reminded herself. There had been no coercion on his part. She'd made love to him because at the time she'd wanted to more than anything else in the world, she admitted honestly.

Don't worry about it, she told herself. She was a grown woman. She was emotionally secure. At least, she'd always thought she was. If she wanted to indulge in a holiday romance with a man full of bullet holes who never seemed to give her a straight answer to any of her questions, then that was her business.

She pulled herself up, wrapped her arms around her legs and, resting her chin on her sandy knees, studied him. He was lying on his back, his arm across his eyes to protect them from the brilliant sunlight. Lovingly, her eyes traced down over his body until her attention was snagged by the ugly red welt of healing flesh that lay in a jagged path across the top of his right thigh. The grayish white color of the sand seemed to accentuate the raw, angry scar left by a bullet ripping a path through his flesh. Where could he have gotten such a wound? No, *two* such wounds. Her eye instinctively moved to his forearm. What kind of company did he keep that left him open to such attacks?

Don't ask, she ordered herself. He won't answer, and it will just ruin the moment. Later, away from the emotionally charged atmosphere that seemed to hang around them like a cloud, she could try to ask him about it.

Cassie clutched a handful of sand and slowly let it trickle over his bare chest. "I always wanted to bury someone in the sand," she said, watching in fascination as the grayish granules stuck to his sweat-dampened skin.

He chuckled. "An interesting fantasy, but not one of mine. Nor is getting caught naked on the beach." He lifted his head and looked around, relaxing slightly when he saw that the shore was still deserted except for the screaming gulls fighting over the remains of their lunch.

Cassie sighed regretfully, knowing he was right. While it was unlikely, someone from the inn might decide to take a walk. Such as Smith. The thought gave her the impetus to move. "We'd better get dressed."

"Unfortunate, but true." He got to his feet with an awkwardness that worried Cassie. Had their lovemaking reinjured his leg? She bit back the question. Dan wouldn't appreciate her harping on his physical limitations.

Instead, she quickly pulled on her clothes while surreptitiously watching him dress.

"What'd you spike that coffee with?" Dan asked slowly.

Cassie blinked, uncertain of his meaning. "Just cream and sugar. Why?"

"Look." He pointed toward the remains of their lunch. A sea gull was staggering away from the now-empty cup of coffee she'd poured for Dan. As they watched, it collapsed and, with one last twitch, was ominously quiet.

Cassie hurried over to it with Dan a step behind her. "Maybe it choked on a sandwich?" she offered.

"A sea gull?" Dan gently picked it up. It hung limply in his hands. "It's dead," he muttered, instinctively looking around.

"Dead?" Cassie repeated, her eyes following his. There was no one to be seen. "But what could have killed it?" She picked up a crust from one of the sandwiches and looked at it closely. Other than being coated with sand, it appeared normal.

Dan set the gull down on the sand and picked up the cup it had been drinking from. He sniffed the dregs in the bottom.

"What is it?" Cassie demanded at his arrested expression.

"I'm not sure, but I think..." He took the thermos and, opening it, sniffed again.

Cassie grabbed it from him and breathed in the strange odor. "What is that smell?" She started to taste it, but Dan jerked the thermos out of her hands.

"Don't do that!" he cried, his sense of guilt and frustration making him curt. "It smells like bitter almonds."

"Bitter... You mean, like in cyanide?" she asked incredulously.

"Like in cyanide." He restoppered the thermos.

"But where...? Garden chemicals," she muttered. "In Agatha Christie mysteries, the gardening stuff is always full of poisons."

"And you do have a large garden." Dan encouraged her line of thought even though he had his doubts.

"And, more important, we also have a spoiled little boy on the premises," Cassie said slowly.

"And you think Brett may have put cyanide into the coffee as a joke?"

Cassie frowned. "I don't know. More likely he took something out of one of the containers in the gardening shed and put it in the sugar bowl, and I put it in the coffee. He probably just thought it would taste terrible. He couldn't know the stuff was poisonous. And we're always having trouble with kids putting salt in the sugar bowls."

"Maybe," Dan said, fearing that there was more to this than merely a spoiled brat with bad taste in practical jokes. He rubbed the back of his neck in frustration. But a hit man made even less sense than a bratty kid. Hit men used guns, not chancy things like poison. They were quick, precise and efficient. Cyanide in the coffee was none of those things.

Maybe Cassie was right, he told himself, desperately trying to believe it. Because the alternative was that he himself was responsible for bringing danger to Cassie. And she was far too important to him to risk exposing her to a hit man. In fact, he thought as he watched her carefully scoop out a hole in the sand to bury the gull, she was fast becoming the single most important thing in his life.

"We'll bury this poor bird, and then we'd better get back and empty out all the sugar bowls. And I want to see what's available in the garden shed for use in creating mayhem," she said. "Please don't mention this to Aunt Hannah. I don't want to worry her."

There was no reason to worry Aunt Hannah, Dan thought grimly. He was plenty worried enough for both of them. And when he told Justin...

No, he decided, he wasn't going to do that. Justin would use this incident as an excuse for them to leave. And he wasn't ready to leave, Dan thought with a sideways glance at Cassie. He wasn't ready to leave at all.

# Seven

"Careful." Dan grabbed Cassie's arm as she tripped over a half-buried seashell in her haste to get back to the house. Her skin felt slightly chilled from the sharp breeze off the ocean and Dan wanted to rub it. To warm it to tingling life as her body had warmed his a short time earlier. Desire slammed through him at the intoxicating memory. Making love to Cassie had been the most fantastic experience of his life. For a brief, tantalizing time he'd been enmeshed in a world of sensation he'd only dimly perceived before. He wanted to shout his discovery to the world. To publicly claim Cassie as his own.

But he couldn't do that. His innate sense of caution overrode the impulse for two reasons: he didn't know exactly how deeply her feelings for him went and there was still the problem of Buczek's threats. Threats that had suddenly taken on more substance. Cassie might be convinced that the poisoning of the sea gull was nothing more than a boyish prank gone awry, but he wasn't so sure.

He glanced at Cassie, trying to decide what would be his best course of action. If he told her about Buczek, she might draw back from him. Any rational person would have second thoughts about associating with a man that a gangster wanted to kill. Even if she were willing to take the risk herself, she still might want him to leave China View so as to avoid the unpleasant publicity his being found murdered at the inn would generate. He grimaced. Ghosts might be good for business, but creating them on the premises definitely would not be!

What he needed was time, he thought in frustration. Time for the law to put Buczek behind bars. Time to allow whatever feelings Cassie did have for him to grow into something more substantial, into something that approached his own depth of feelings. And time for him to rethink his present career.

Maybe the time had finally come for him to trade his constant travels around the world for a more-settled existence. For the type of job that would allow him the opportunity to develop and nurture personal relationships. For the kind of job that would allow him to be home nights to put children to bed. *His* children. The thought filled him with an immense satisfaction. Two, he decided. A sturdy little boy with Cassie's gorgeous blue-gray eyes and a small girl with her mother's inquiring mind.

"Let's check the gardening shed first." Cassie's worried voice pulled him out of his thoughts. "I want to see if Agatha Christie was right and any of those gardening supplies really do have cyanide in them."

Motioning for him to be quiet, she crept around the side of the inn with Dan right behind her.

As they passed, Cassie peeked through the multipaned glass windows that lined three of the sun-room's walls. Madam Rowinski was still sitting there knitting something. She was facing the door to the lobby with her back to them. She looked as if she hadn't moved since Cassie had left.

"From where Madam Rowinski's sitting she would have had a clear view of anyone entering the inn," Dan said once they were past the sun-room.

"Or if they went through the lobby to the kitchen. Gertie was cleaning the bedrooms upstairs, so she wouldn't have seen anything."

"Could we ask Madam Rowinski if she noticed anything after we check out the garden shed?" Dan suggested.

"Yes. We just need to figure out a way to ask her if she happened to notice someone adding cyanide to the sugar bowl without making her wonder if it's safe to stay here," Cassie said dryly as she yanked open the shed door.

"Is this shed normally kept unlocked?" Dan asked, glancing around the luxuriant garden. It appeared deserted.

"As far back as I can remember." Cassie stepped into the dusky interior. "Vandalism has never been a problem around here and... What's that?" She pointed to a whitish powder that had been spilled across the top of the potting table. As if someone had been in too much of a hurry to either take care in pouring it or to clean up the spill afterward.

Dan wet his forefinger and dipped it into the substance, then smelled it. "Bitter almonds." He held out his finger.

Cassie leaned closer and sniffed. "Bitter almonds," she agreed. She picked up the open container on the table and read the label. Potassium cyanide was the first ingredient listed.

Cassie rubbed a pinch of it between her fingers. "This looks a little like sugar. Mixed with the real thing, you wouldn't notice. I didn't. And the smell wasn't obvious when it was dry. And..." She leaned over and picked something up off the stone floor.

Brett's slingshot. Dan recognized it with an enormous sense of relief. Cassie had been right; this whole thing was nothing more than a dumb practical joke. Buczek hadn't been behind it.

"You are going to ask the Essels to leave, aren't you?" he demanded.

Cassie tossed the slingshot from one hand to the other as she weighed her options. "No," she finally said.

"No?" he repeated incredulously. "Why not?"

"Think about it for a minute. What am I going to say to his parents? I'm kicking you out because your son tried to poison me?"

"That sounds like a promising beginning to me."

"And when they deny it and ask me what proof I have?" Cassie raised her russet eyebrows. "What do I say then? That he's a brat and I found him messing around in the kitchen? Or I found his slingshot near some spilled potassium cyanide?"

"It's all true," Dan insisted.

"Yeah, but it doesn't prove anything if they should decide to retaliate by suing us, and they're the type that might. They can point out that I didn't really see him do it. And that he could well have dropped the slingshot at any time."

"So what do you intend to do?"

Cassie shrugged impotently. "What I can. I'll empty out every container of sugar we have in the inn. Then I'll tell his parents that under no circumstances is Brett to go into the kitchen. And I'll lock all the gardening chemicals in the basement until after they leave."

Dan ran his fingers around the back of his neck in frustration. "I don't like it, but you're probably right. Why don't we go talk to our resident medium and ask her what she saw?"

"After we get rid of the sugar bowls." Cassie hurried across the peaceful garden and rushed into the kitchen. To her relief, the sugar bowl was exactly where she'd left it. It took only a few minutes to empty all the bowls and load them into the dishwasher.

Satisfied that she'd neutralized the effects of Brett's prank, she went to talk to Madam Rowinski.

"Enjoy your brunch on the beach?" Madam Rowinski gave Cassie a sly smile when she noticed that Dan was with her.

To her embarrassment, Cassie felt a flush scorch her cheeks as she remembered just how much she had enjoyed that interlude. Not even her fright over the cyanide was sufficient to dim the memory.

"Fresh air always gives me an appetite," Cassie muttered. At Dan's muffled choking, she winced. "You ought to take a walk yourself," she continued doggedly. "You'd probably have the whole beach to yourself. I think the Essels have already left."

"Yes, right after you did." Madam Rowinski's nose wrinkled in disgust. "Taking that child with them, thank God! I was hoping that with them out of the way, the ghost would put in an appearance, but no such luck."

"I thought the Essels said that ghosts only come out at dusk and dawn?" Dan offered.

"Amateurs," Madam Rowinski said dismissively. "Why, some of my very best séances have been held in broad daylight."

Dan stared at her, his reporter's curiosity stirred. "Would you be willing to do a séance here?"

"Perhaps, if the aura is agreeable," Madam Rowinski murmured noncommittally. "Some spirits object to being compelled, and I wouldn't want to risk offending Jonas."

"No, indeed," Cassie agreed wholeheartedly as she left the room. She had enough to worry about. A séance would only add to the general mayhem.

"I think I'll go see if Smith saw anyone hanging around the shed," Dan said as he followed Cassie into the lobby.

"I thought you didn't know him!" Cassie exclaimed.

"Of course I know him. I met him yesterday," Dan said, not wanting to lie to Cassie but seeing no viable alternative.

The truth about his relationship with Smith would lead to other truths. Some of which he most emphatically didn't want to tell her.

"You were arguing with him on the beach earlier," Cassie reminded him. "Maybe he did it. Maybe we've been blaming the obvious suspect and overlooking the subtle one. Maybe your Mr. Smith did it to get even with you for the argument. He could have put the poison in the sugar while I was upstairs telling Gertie that I was going for a walk."

Dan shook his head emphatically. "Smith would never for one moment consider murder."

"And how do you know that if you only met him yesterday?" Cassie challenged.

"I've seen his wardrobe. He'd never do anything to land himself in jail. They don't wear custom-tailored clothes in prison."

A rueful smile curved her lips. "You're probably right. Not that I really think he did it. Putting something in the sugar bowl is a childish piece of spite. And most likely committed by a child."

"I'll still pump Smith. If he did see Brett do it, we'll have proof and can chuck the little monster out. In the meantime..." Dan grasped her chin between his fingers and lifted her head. His breath wafted across her mouth, making the soft flesh tingle with anticipation.

She didn't have long to anticipate. Dan leaned forward, and his lips found hers with devastating accuracy.

Cassie sighed at the sense of homecoming that wrapped around her. She wanted to consign Brett and his mischief making to perdition and disappear somewhere with Dan. Somewhere private where they could explore all the fantastic feelings he so effortlessly aroused in her. But to her massive disappointment, instead of deepening the kiss, he raised his head and smiled down at her.

"Something on account," he murmured, and whistling happily, he limped up the stairs.

Bemused, Cassie watched until he'd disappeared from sight. He needed cosseting, she thought. Even more than that, he needed to be kept out of the line of any more gunfire.

Maybe he was in the military, she considered as she slowly walked back to the kitchen. Or maybe he'd simply been a tourist in Washington. What had that newspaper article she'd read yesterday called it? Murder capital of the United States?

Cassie pushed open the swinging door into the kitchen and froze when she heard a muffled thump from the pantry. Cautiously she crept across the room and peeked inside...to find Jonas happily pulling a tin of fruitcake off the top shelf.

"Just the man I want to see," Cassie said.

"I wanted to see you, too. Do you know that little varmint took the last of the cookies?" he complained.

Cassie grinned. "Beat you to them, did he? Never mind the cookies, I want to ask you about something. Did you see Brett put anything in the sugar bowl?"

"Nope." Jonas looked up from his efforts to pry open the cake tin. "I was busy elsewhere." The lid finally came loose, sending a wave of brandy fumes into the air. "Ah." Jonas breathed deeply, an ecstatic smile on his face. He broke off a piece of cake and popped it in his mouth. "What'd the little varmint put in the sugar bowl? Salt?"

"No, potassium cyanide."

Jonas choked and looked down at the fruitcake suspiciously.

"Don't worry," Cassie assured him. "Brett can't reach that high. Besides, he wouldn't have had time. As it was, he had to have been pretty quick."

Thoughtfully, Jonas ate another morsel as he considered her words. Finally, he said, "It doesn't seem likely."

"What doesn't?"

"That the little varmint did that." Jonas scratched his beard thoughtfully. "From what I've seen, he's the kind of kid who would want to be there to enjoy the havoc he caused."

Cassie frowned. There was a certain amount of truth to that. But if Jonas was right, then who had done it? Smith?

"Jonas, what about Smith?"

"A man-miller if ever I saw one."

"Man-miller?" Cassie didn't understand the term even if there was no mistaking the contempt with which it was uttered.

"You know, a dandy. A maw worm who's always concerned with his looks. Not a real man," Jonas said scornfully.

"There are lots of different kinds of men in the world, and they don't all have to have dirt under their fingernails to be real," Cassie pointed out.

"Smith's got no bottom," Jonas insisted. "Wouldn't want him on my ship. Ha! Turned green and shrieked like an old maid when I did no more than materialize in front of him."

"Careful there, friend. Some of us old maids are sensitive about our status."

"You could have that Mr. Travis if'n you were to go about it right," Jonas suggested slyly.

Cassie stared at him for a long moment and then, unable to resist the temptation, asked, "And what would be the right way to go about it?"

"Play up to him. He's feeling real restless. Like he's at a turning point in his life." Jonas pursed his lips thoughtfully. "Spends a lot of time staring at the wall and thinking. Bet he's thinking about the future. No reason you couldn't be a part of his future, nice gal like you."

Cassie watched as he broke off another piece of fruitcake. She wasn't sure exactly what Jonas did when he wasn't acting, but whatever it was had made him a shrewd judge of character. And very observant. Could he be right about Dan? *Was* he at a turning point in his life? And was that turning point somehow tied up with the bullet wounds in his leg and arm? And where did Smith fit into this, because she was willing to bet her last dollar that he did somewhere.

Cassie sighed. What she needed were a few answers, and what she'd gotten were more questions.

"Do you think your aunt would mind if'n I were to take the rest of the fruitcake?" Jonas eyed it covetously.

"I doubt if she'd even notice it was gone. Help yourself, and don't forget your money." She retrieved the envelope from the shelf and handed it to him.

Jonas carelessly shoved it into his coat pocket.

"You want I should put the fear of God into that little varmint?" he asked.

"Tempting, but it's more likely the little varmint would do you an injury. Let's content ourselves to keeping out of his way. Although maybe if you were to give his parents a showing, they might leave to report back to whatever group they belong to?"

"They have very strange ideas about ghosts," Jonas said disparagingly. "Seem to think they come draped in sheets and the like." He shook his head in disgust.

"No sheets," Cassie said quickly. "They're too expensive to be cutting holes in. Besides, you're liable to trip and blow your cover."

"Maybe." Jonas clutched the cake tin to his rusty black vest and ambled out the back door with a calculating expression on his hairy face that increased Cassie's feeling of unease.

She sank down in a kitchen chair and heaved a heartfelt sigh. As a peaceful vacation, her time at China View was a flop. But as a romantic encounter... A dreamy expression muted the blue of her eyes. It was well on its way to surpassing every fantasy she'd ever had.

And Jonas claimed she could get Dan on a permanent basis, she remembered. But did she want him on a permanent basis? When you got right down to it, she didn't know one solid fact about either Dan's profession or his background. A tremor of uncertainty ruffled her pleasure in her memories of their lovemaking.

But she had a very clear reading on his personality. She relaxed slightly. She knew he had a sharp, incisive mind. That he made enough money to be able to afford hand-tailored jackets from England, but that he didn't care enough about fashion to replace them when they became slightly threadbare. That he had a dry sense of humor that neatly dovetailed her own. That he was a fantastic lover who cared about giving pleasure as well as receiving it. And that he was lonely.

Dan Travis was a man who gave the impression of being a loner. A lonely loner, she amended, remembering his revealing comment about how he envied her relationship with Aunt Hannah and the security of knowing everyone in Levington. But he was also the type of man who went after what he wanted. So if he really envied her her family ties, then why hadn't he set about forging some of his own? Even if he were leery of tying himself to a long-term relationship with a woman, community ties were easy to make and maintain.

Cassie sighed. Yet more questions to which she had no answers. And she wasn't likely to get any sitting here day-dreaming, she told herself as she got to her feet. She had other things she needed to do. Such as removing every gardening concoction from the shed and locking it in the basement before Brett got back.

"Tell me, does the inestimable Ms. Whitney count gardening among her many talents?" Justin watched from his bedroom window as Cassie crossed the garden toward the shed.

"Why?" Dan asked.

"Because she's sneaking through the flowers in what could only be described as a furtive manner," he said. "Almost as if she didn't want anyone to know what she was doing." He turned around and stared thoughtfully at Dan. "If I were the one responsible for that magnificent garden, I'd want everyone to know about it."

"Ah, but then you never were the least bit shy about taking credit," Dan countered warily. He'd come up to try to get information from Justin, not to give him any. Especially not the information that he'd almost been poisoned.

Justin would be very upset if he were to get himself killed, even accidentally, Dan thought wryly. Harry would never release him from his contract then.

"If you don't blow your own horn, no one else will," Justin said seriously. "Look at you. One of the most respected men in journalism and what have you done with it?" He shook his head in exasperation. "Nothing. In your shoes, I'd at least be an anchor in New York City or L.A., if not pushing Peter Jennings for his job."

"But I don't want Jennings' job," Dan said. "I can think of nothing more boring than sitting in a studio repeating news other people have dug out."

"But think of the money that's involved," Justin argued. "Think of the power you'd have. People believe what they hear on the news."

"More's the pity."

Justin shrugged. "Maybe, but to get back to my original question, why is our hostess sneaking through the garden? In fact, what do you really know about her?" Justin's face hardened.

"Have you been watching old movie reruns?" Dan scoffed. "Cassie Whitney is an advertising-account executive at Welton and Mitchell in the city. She just helps her aunt here at China View during vacations."

"Oh!" Justin sounded nonplussed. "Well, you must admit her actions out there are suspicious."

"Not any more suspicious than two grown men hiding out in New Hampshire and seeing bogeymen behind every door!"

"If that is a reference to my seeing that ghost last night—" Justin began hotly.

"Not at all. I don't blame you for being startled. I was the first time I saw him, too."

"I wasn't startled. I was terrified," Justin admitted grudgingly. "And I still don't know how he did it. He just seemed to appear. One minute he was there, and the next he was gone."

Dan shook his head. "No, one minute you weren't paying attention and the next you were. That's the way con artists work. I imagine Madam Rowinski does her séances the same way."

Justin frowned. "You think she's mixed up with the ghost?"

Dan shook his head. "No, I think Cassie hired the ghost to provide a little judicious haunting."

Justin's eyes narrowed. "She is in advertising."

"And as sharp as they come. Business here at the inn was down. What could be simpler than for her to spread a rumor about a ghost being sighted, all the while insisting that there is no such thing as a ghost and there must be some perfectly reasonable explanation?"

Justin smiled reluctantly. "You know, I can almost admire the plan. At least, I could if I hadn't been taken in by it." He grimaced self-consciously. "She probably thinks I'm a fool."

"No, she probably thinks you were helping the cause along by pretending to be frightened," Dan said, liking Justin much better when he was uncertain than when he was acting like the final authority on everything. "Have you been up here since you got back from your run?" he asked.

"Almost. I made the mistake of going into the sun-room first. Madam Rowinski was there waiting for victims. I told her I had a headache and came up here. I saw Ms. Whitney go out with a picnic basket." He was about to add a ribald comment, but the expression on Dan's face made him think better of it. "And after she disappeared down the beach in your direction, the Essels and their walking advertisement for birth control left. Then nothing happened until you came up. Why?" he asked.

"No particular reason," Dan lied. "I just wondered if anyone suspicious had shown up."

"Well, the hit man obviously hasn't registered at the inn. In this group he'd stick out like a sore thumb."

"True." Dan relaxed at Justin's logic. The cyanide had really been nothing more than a stupid prank by a spoiled brat. He didn't have anything to worry about.

# Eight

Cassie looked up from the cooking pans she was drying, trying to identify the strange sounds she could hear coming from the back porch. Her first thought was that Brett was up to more devilment, but then she realized that it couldn't be. He'd left the inn with his parents immediately after breakfast, and they weren't expected back until dinner. If they came back.

The Essels had made it embarrassingly obvious to everyone at breakfast that morning that they'd deeply resented Cassie's request that they confine their son to the public areas of the inn. Clearly, their sense of outrage was only slightly less intense than their desire to make contact with Jonas. It remained to be seen which would win out in the end.

Curiously, she watched as the door opened and Jonas backed into the kitchen, dragging something behind him.

"Are those tire chains?" she asked in confusion.

"Logging chains." He pulled the last of them over the doorsill with a jerk. "They're thicker."

Cassie walked over and peered down at the massive links. "Dirtier, too. Why are you lugging logging chains around?"

"Because you won't let me use sheets."

Cassie stared at him. "I fail to see the connection."

"For haunting. You see," he continued at her puzzled look, "people seem to expect a few furbelows, and since you wouldn't let me use sheets, I borrowed these chains. I thought I'd drag them around the upstairs hall and moan a little."

"I'm the one who's going to be moaning if you do that," Cassie said tartly, "and it won't be a little bit, either. Those things are coated with dirt and oil."

"It adds to the authenticity," Jonas assured her.

"What it'll add to is my work load!"

"Mustn't do that." Jonas covetously eyed the fresh apple pies cooling on the counter. "Cooking's more important than chains."

Cassie chuckled. "Food's more important than anything to you. I baked one of them just for you."

Jonas beamed happily at her. "That's right kind of you, gal." He hurriedly got a fork and a plate, sat down at the table and pulled one of the pies toward him. "Nothing like a piece of fresh apple pie to put heart in a man. It's even better with cream."

Cassie responded to his hopeful look by fetching the coffee cream from the refrigerator.

He poured some over his generous slab of pastry and took a bite. An ecstatic smile curved his lips. "Perfect," he pronounced. "That Dan Travis is one lucky man to get himself a gal who can not only cook, but is sharp as a tack in the bargain."

"Don't jump to conclusions. Dan hasn't asked me to marry him. Hasn't even hinted yet." A wistful note unconsciously crept into her voice, a fact she immediately denied when she heard it. She didn't know enough about Dan Travis to be thinking in terms of permanency, she lectured herself.

It didn't matter that when she'd made love to Dan she'd felt as if she'd just discovered the secret of the universe. What mattered was that his background was a closed book to her. He refused to trust her enough to be open with her, to tell her the truth about how he had been injured. To explain the bullet wounds. To explain why he knew so little about insurance, and why Ed was able to blackmail him into writing an editorial. And without trust there could be no possibility of a long-term relationship between them. Trust was the one thing she absolutely had to have in a permanent relationship.

Although maybe she could continue to see him once they'd returned to New York, and trust would somehow develop.... Provided he really *was* headquartered in New York and that that wasn't just another of his fabrications. She stifled a sigh.

Concentrate on the present, she encouraged herself. On what they had going for them here and now. Because even flawed as it was by Dan's lack of openness, it was still the most exciting relationship she'd ever been involved in.

"That was superb." Jonas licked his fork clean and then set it down on his empty plate.

"Thank you. If you're finished with your snack, would you please take those chains back to wherever it was you got them?"

Jonas shook his head regretfully as he gathered them up. "Seems a real pity. I could have done a good job with them."

"Cassie?" Dan's raised voice echoed from right outside the door leading to the lobby. "Are you in the kitchen?"

Cassie instinctively started to answer him and then stopped when she remembered Jonas. Dan mustn't find him here. Not that she thought he really believed Jonas was a ghost, but having doubts was one thing, finding the supposed ghost sitting in her kitchen snacking was quite another.

"Jonas," she whispered as she turned around. To her relief, he was already gone. He must have hurried out the back door the moment he'd heard Dan's voice. Jonas was getting pretty good with his disappearing act, she thought approvingly. He'd even managed to keep those chains from clanking.

"I'm in here," she called.

The door was suddenly pushed open, and Dan limped into the kitchen, bringing an aura of vibrancy with him. He seemed to radiate kinetic energy, she thought as she eagerly studied his face. His eyes gleamed with suppressed emotion, although exactly what emotion, she wasn't sure. Definitely a happy one, though. Cassie felt her own spirits soar as he grinned at her. Fascinated, she watched as the skin at the corners of his eyes crinkled enticingly, giving her a glimpse of an elusive dimple in his left cheek.

Dan Travis was glad to see her. No, she amended as she watched the pupils of his eyes darken. He was *very* glad to see her. And somehow that knowledge made all the petty irritations of her hectic morning evaporate, to be replaced by a sense of anticipation. The day suddenly held boundless possibilities.

"I found your aunt upstairs in the linen closet as I was leaving my room," Dan said.

Cassie grimaced. "She's probably hiding from Madam Rowinski. That woman could talk a tape recorder to a standstill."

"There are a lot more pitfalls to running an inn than I would have thought." He absently picked up a tiny piece of crust Jonas had broken off and munched on it. "Does your aunt have to take in paying guests?"

"No. At least, not if she'd accept some help from me. But she won't take a penny."

"Then what she needs is a more congenial class of guest," Dan suggested.

"Or to win the lottery, which is about as likely," Cassie said dryly. "What may I do for you?"

"Well, since you ask..." Dan suddenly reached out and pulled her into his arms.

Taken off guard, Cassie stumbled slightly, falling against him. She clutched his shoulders to steady herself and took a deep breath, breathing in his intoxicating scent. He smelled warm and musky, and she instinctively nestled closer to him.

Her breasts tingled where they were squashed against his chest. She felt light-headed, dizzy with anticipation as his lips swooped down on hers with devastating accuracy. His warm mouth covered hers with a hunger he made no effort to hide. Dan Travis wanted her, and the knowledge fed her own desire.

She snuggled closer, fitting her soft body more securely against his much harder one. Her eyes drifted shut, closing out reality in order to better concentrate on his kiss.

She felt the tip of his tongue moving against her lips like a brand. Instinctively, her mouth opened, and she shivered violently as his tongue took advantage of her invitation to surge inside. His arms tightened convulsively and, with a slow thoroughness that seemed at odds with the tension she could feel tightening his muscles, he explored the velvety softness of her inner cheek.

Cassie clutched the thick cotton of his sweater, her fingertips digging into the firm muscles of his shoulders beneath. Compulsively, she pressed closer still, trying to intensify the sensation growing in her. She wanted the feeling to go on and on and never stop.

She felt an overwhelming sense of loss when Dan lifted his head and stared down into her unfocused eyes. He leaned his forehead against hers and whispered, "We have to stop this."

"Why?" she muttered as she captured the taut flesh of his lower lip between her teeth and began to nibble on it. A small, satisfied smile curved her lips as she felt the shudder that lanced through him.

"I have things to do."

"Me, too." Cassie gently bit down on his lip.

"Do you have any idea what that does to me?" he muttered. "I want to find the nearest bed and make mad, passionate love to you."

"What a lack of imagination you have," Cassie taunted, her tongue flickering out to caress where her teeth had been seconds before. "Haven't you heard? Beds are passé."

He groaned as she slipped her hand beneath his sweater and ran her palm up over his bare chest.

He captured her wandering hand in his. "Someone might walk in on us."

"No," Cassie murmured as she nuzzled her face against his neck, reveling in the raspy, silken texture of his skin. "I already fed him."

"Fed who?" Dan asked.

She lifted her head and shook it slightly in an attempt to dispel the sensual spell that held her in thrall. Careful, she warned herself. Dan doesn't know about Jonas. Not really.

"The handyman. He left a few minutes ago."

"Which is what I should be doing." He straightened up. "I just came to tell you that Ed called. He needs the final version of that editorial this afternoon."

Cassie bit her lip to hold back her instinctive objection. She'd been working at breakneck speed ever since early this morning in the hope that she'd be able to spend the afternoon with Dan, and now she found that he was planning to leave.

"I asked your aunt whether she minded if I asked you to go into town with me, and she said she was more than capable of running the inn by herself."

"She is, too," Cassie promptly agreed as a sense of pleasurable expectation bubbled through her. It wasn't a whole afternoon alone with Dan as she'd hoped, but she would be with him. Not only that, but there was the ride into town and back. A secretive smile tugged at the corners of her mouth. They'd be alone in the car, and it was a very desolate road between China View and Levington. There would be no one to notice if they were to park for a while.

Cassie brushed her tousled curls back and tucked her yellow silk blouse into her beige linen shorts.

"Aunt Hannah won't mind if I take the Packard," she said.

"That's okay. I'll drive," Dan said. "I might as well get some use out of the unlimited mileage on my rental car."

Unlimited mileage, Cassie thought dreamily as she followed Dan out of the kitchen. With unlimited mileage they could go anywhere.

"Going out?" Madam Rowinski called to them from the sun-room as they passed.

"Yes," Dan called back, speeding up slightly.

Cassie paused momentarily and gave Madam Rowinski a friendly smile. At the moment, she felt friendly toward everyone, even compulsive talkers.

She caught up with Dan at his rental car. She climbed in and absently fastened the seat belt as she glanced around the parking area. Madam Rowinski's car was there, but Smith's was gone.

"What's the matter?" Dan asked as he headed toward the cliff road that led to town.

"Nothing," she said slowly. "I just hadn't realized that Smith had left the inn. I wonder where he went?"

"Probably sight-seeing," Dan said dismissively, and Cassie studied him out of the corner of her eye.

Why did Dan always downplay her curiosity about Smith? The question nagged at her. Dan was a very curious man. It permeated his whole personality. But he wasn't the least bit curious about Smith. Why? She didn't know. And when she was with Dan, the reason didn't seem as important as when she wasn't, she conceded. When she was with him, her thoughts couldn't seem to get beyond the fact that she wanted to kiss him and make love to him. But how long would that last? she wondered uneasily. When would the fact that she knew so little about Dan's background begin to assume more importance in her mind? Begin to crowd out the intense pleasure she felt in his presence?

"Maybe the poor man is hiding out after his encounter with the ghost the other night," Dan added at her worried expression, knowing full well that Smith had gone out to find a fax machine to send in a story he was working on for the paper.

"There is no such thing as a ghost," she automatically replied.

"Then perhaps you could tell me what Smith saw. Or for that matter, what I saw." Dan tightened his grip on the steering wheel as the road began to narrow along the edge of the cliff.

"Mass hallucination?" Cassie suggested. "Perhaps your Mr. Smith is a closet drinker? Maybe he goes to out-of-the-way inns to drink himself into a stupor every night, and he had already started when he thought he saw something?"

Dan snorted. "Not a chance. Overindulgence in liquor would ruin his looks and . . ."

Cassie glanced over at him, frowning at the sight of his knuckles gleaming whitely from the force of the pressure he was exerting on the steering wheel. His face looked unexpectedly strained, as if the skin had been stretched too tightly over his bones. A sudden premonition of impending disaster sliced through her.

"What's the matter?" she demanded as the car began to pick up speed on the steep grade.

"Something's wrong with the brakes," he said slowly.

Cassie closed her eyes as the enormity of that simple statement churned through her disbelieving mind. If the brakes failed entirely... She glanced out the window at the sheer drop off the cliff edge to the sea and swallowed, sick with terror. They would hurtle over the side to... To their deaths, most likely. As little traveled as this road was, it might be days before someone stumbled across the car. She caught her lower lip between her teeth to stop her instinctive protest.

She turned in her seat and stared at Dan, trying to imprint the memory of his features in her mind for all eternity...because she loved him. Impending disaster crystalized her confused emotions into a single, coherent thought. She loved Dan Travis. She didn't know where he'd come from or where he was going, but nonetheless, she loved him.

With monumental effort, she sealed her discovery away in the back of her mind and forced herself to focus on their present problem. "If we can just hold the road for about a quarter of a mile, we'll reach the level stretch along the beach," she told him.

"Right," Dan said grimly.

As she watched, he switched off the engine and pulled on the emergency brake. The car slowed it precipitous downward flight, but it also jerked sharply toward the edge of the cliff, almost as if it were a live entity determined to take them to their deaths.

Dan fought fiercely to maintain control of the car, his face a mask of intense concentration. Cassie huddled on the seat, trying not to distract him. He seemed to know what he was doing. Whether it would work or not remained to be seen.

He managed to hold the car on the road for almost a thousand feet, and just when Cassie was beginning to think that they'd reach the level stretch that hugged the shoreline, the car gave a violent jerk and swerved sharply to the right.

Cassie braced her feet against the floor, grabbed the door handle and hung on as she car slid over the shoulder of the road. It crashed through a thick stand of wild beach plums, swung wildly around and came to a precipitous stop when its left rear fender smashed against a huge gray boulder.

Cassie gulped and then dragged a deep breath into her lungs. It didn't help to slow her racing heart. She felt disoriented, nauseous and scared to death.

"We were almost killed!" She swallowed at the sour taste of panicked fear. "If you hadn't known what to do...we'd have just kept picking up speed and..." She pressed trembling fingers over her quivering eyelids and made a determined effort to get control of herself. There was no need for her to spell it out. Dan had eyes. He could see. But did he? The question surfaced through her muddled fears. Could Dan see what was happening?

Yesterday they'd almost been poisoned and today almost squashed. She looked at him. He was slumped behind the steering wheel, his head resting against the side window. His skin had a grayish cast to it, and his lips were clenched together. In fear? Or in anger? She didn't know, but she could empathize with either emotion.

"Dan?" To her dismay, her voice broke in a sob.

He opened his eyes and slowly turned toward her, his movements awkward and clumsy. He maneuvered himself out from under the steering wheel and blindly reached for her, yanking her into his arms. He pressed her head into his shoulder and rubbed his shaking fingers down over her cheek as if trying to reassure himself that she was still alive.

Frantically, Cassie burrowed closer as reaction set in and she started to shake uncontrollably.

"Don't," he muttered. "It's all right."

"All right?" Her voice rose hysterically despite her efforts to control it. "We were almost poisoned yesterday and today we've almost dropped off the side of a cliff and you tell me it's all right? Why don't you try telling me that it's a coincidence?''

Dan's jagged chuckle had no roots in humor. ''Would you believe me if I did?''

''No,'' she said baldly. ''Dan, what the hell is going on?'' Her teeth began to chatter.

''Ah, Cassie, darling, don't.'' He lowered his head and captured her mouth. There was no gentleness in his kiss, only a frantic need to reaffirm that he was alive.

It was a need Cassie shared. Convulsively, her arms closed around his neck and she strained against him. They had come so close to never sharing this again. A violent shudder racked her, and his own arms tightened, molding her even closer to him.

''Oh, Cassie,'' he muttered against her lips. ''I think—''

''Don't think.'' Her fingers clenched the back of his head, and she pulled his mouth to hers once more. She didn't want to think, to weigh implications. She wanted to kiss him. To caress his warm body. To experience the emotions that only this man could make her feel.

Hastily, she unbuttoned her blouse and then yanked his sweater up over his head, craving yet more physical contact. Heat seemed to pour off his bare chest, and she pressed her lace-covered breasts against him, trying to warm her own chilled body. For a moment the sensation of his hot flesh was enough, and then it wasn't. She needed more to beat back the specter of what had almost happened.

As if he could read her mind and agreed with her conclusions, Dan reached around her and unfastened her bra with fingers that shook under the force of the emotions driving him.

He pulled her bra free and tossed it into the back seat and then pulled her pliant body against him once more.

Cassie breathed a sigh of exquisite pleasure as the sensitive tips of her breasts were crushed into the burning heat of his chest. He felt so warm. She snuggled closer, nestling her face under his chin and shuddering at the feel of his skin scraping abrasively over her forehead. She took a deep breath, the better to savor the masculine scent that clung to him. He smelled of an astringent soap, musky cologne and other far-more-elusive aromas. Scents that excited her unbearably.

She reached up and ran the palm of her hand over his lean cheek, her fingers instinctively searching for the elusive dimple she'd glimpsed earlier.

"My God, Cassie." Dan's hoarse voice fed her excitement.

He reached around her and fumbled with something on the side of her seat. Cassie squeaked in surprise as her seat suddenly gave way and she found herself lying on her back with him looming above her. She stared up into his hot brown eyes, watching the swirling, golden flecks in them gather speed with the strength of his emotions. She could spend the rest of her life watching those mysterious flecks of color, she thought dreamily. Then she shivered as she realized the rest of her life had almost been measured in seconds.

"My precious one," Dan murmured. He stared down at her and the glow in his eyes seemed to intensify. He obviously found her very desirable, and the knowledge bubbled through her veins like vintage champagne. It made her feel omnipotent. Capable of anything.

Confidently, she reached out and grasped the back of his neck, intending to pull him close enough to kiss him again. But he locked his forearms, resisting the pressure. Instead, he slowly lowered himself toward her and lightly rubbed his hair-covered chest across the sensitive tips of her breasts.

Cassie gasped as reaction raced through her. She could feel her breasts swelling, her nipples convulsing into tight buds. Restlessly, she moved under the force of the emotions gathering in her.

"Ah, Cassie," he muttered. "You're so beautiful. The most beautiful thing I've ever seen." He reverently encircled her small breast in his hand, kneading it with his fingers as if he found the texture irresistible. "Like a Michelangelo statue of the finest pale pink marble, except that you're real—real and warm—and you smell of roses." He buried his head between her breasts, and Cassie trembled at the scratchy feel of his cheeks against her sensitive skin.

"So beautiful," he muttered. "So alive." He leaned forward and lightly outlined the dark, dusky flesh of her nipple with the tip of his tongue.

"Dan!" she gasped as a fiery sensation seemed to shoot from her breast to her abdomen. His breath seared her tormented flesh, increasing her sense of agitated urgency to a fever pitch. When he captured her nipple in his hot mouth and suckled, Cassie frantically clutched at his head, holding him tightly to her. The urgency in her body was escalating, pushing aside rational thought. It left no room for any concern other than her need to make love to him, of having his heated warmth within her. Of releasing the tormented urgency that gripped her.

"I need you so much," Dan muttered as he fumbled with his belt buckle. Once he'd managed to free it, he unzipped his pants and, bracing himself against the steering wheel, shrugged out of them.

Greedily, Cassie stared at his magnificent body, reveling in the powerful muscles that underlay his bronzed skin. She swallowed in longing, knowing how those muscles could act on her own much-softer ones. She craved the feel of his body against her, on top of her, inside her, and she didn't think she could wait any longer. She needed him now. All time seemed to have telescoped into this moment. There was no future nor any past. No danger or fear, just a seemingly inexhaustible whirlpool of desire that stretched to fill her every pore.

"Dan," she murmured, "make love to me."

"I will," he vowed. There was an odd note to his voice that in a more rational frame of mind Cassie might have wondered at, but now all that she could think about was the need to get closer to him.

Impatiently, she unzipped her shorts and then raised her hips as he yanked them and her satin panties off, letting them fall unheeded to the floor.

Driven by a need that matched her own, he nudged his knee between her legs and then slipped between her thighs.

Cassie took a deep breath, quivering as she breathed in the increasingly musky scent pouring off Dan's body. Blindly she encircled his waist with her arms and pulled him down, at the same time pushing her heels into the floor and forcing her hips upward, against his throbbing flesh.

The result was instantaneous. Dan moved forward, encasing himself in her hot body. Cassie squeezed her eyes shut, the better to concentrate on the emotion flowing along her nerve endings like wildfire burning out of control. As he moved forward and slowly withdrew, only to repeat the exquisite motion, the tension encircling Cassie's body built to an unbearable pitch. Just when she thought she couldn't stand it any longer, it snapped, hurtling her into a rainbow-hued world where only sensation held any meaning. She swung through it in ever-slowing arcs, absorbing the pleasure as she moved, until finally the momentum eased and she was aware of being protectively covered by Dan's boneless body.

Cassie snuggled her cheek against his damp chest and breathed in the warm, masculine scent of his body in a vain attempt to shut out the memories crowding to the front of her mind now that her passion had waned. She didn't want to think about what had almost happened, but neither could she ignore it. What was the old saying? Third time's the charm? If they didn't uncover whoever was behind these inexplicable attacks...

She took a deep breath. She had to know what she wa
facing and why. And the only one who could tell her was
Dan.

"Dan?" she murmured.

"Mmm?" His breath was a soft pressure against her face.

"What happened?" She frowned as she felt his muscles
clench in sudden tension. Why? Because he was remembering what had happened or why it had happened?

He moved away from her, and Cassie watched with a
feeling of profound loss as he struggled into his clothes in
the cramped front seat. What dismayed her more was the
closed expression on his face—as if he knew something,
something he had no intention of sharing. Cassie felt like
screaming in frustration as he forced open the door on his
side and climbed out of the car. How could she love him so
wholeheartedly and yet know so little about him?

But she was going to find out, she vowed grimly as she
hastily scrambled into her own clothes and followed him.

She watched as Dan walked around to the rear of the car
and inspected the damage their collision with the boulder
had done. One thing was certain, she thought grimly. This
couldn't possibly be blamed on Brett. He didn't know
enough to disable a car.

Dan tried to pry open the trunk, and when it wouldn't
budge, he silently walked to the front of the car. Lying down
on the sand, he inched himself underneath the vehicle. A
second later Cassie heard his muffled explanation, followed by a very impressive string of curses as he slowly
wiggled back out.

"What is it?" Cassie peered at the liquid gleaming on his
fingers.

"Brake fluid," he said curtly as he cleaned his hand on a
tuft of dried grass.

"From the cut in the brake line." She leapt to the obvious conclusion.

"How did you..." His reaction was all the confirmation she needed.

Cassie shivered. Things like this happened in New York City, not in sleepy little Levington. And they most certainly happened to other people, not to her. She stared at him for a long moment and then asked, "Why is someone trying to kill you?"

"Don't be melodramatic."

"Melodramatic?" she sputtered. "I have been in the middle of two attempted murders, and the only reason I'm here to complain about it is because the murderer is not very adept at his chosen profession. And you tell me not to be melodramatic? What does it take to get your attention? A bullet-riddled body?"

"It would certainly be more in character," Dan said obliquely. "Come on. We'll walk into town and call the garage from Ed's."

He started to climb up the incline back to the road. Cassie watched his halting progress with a sense of acute frustration. It was a good mile into town and she wasn't at all sure he should be walking that far on his injured leg. Especially not after the pounding it had received in the crash. But on the other hand... She glanced nervously up and down the deserted road. It might be more dangerous to leave him behind while she went for help. Whoever had cut that brake line might decide to check on the results of his handiwork.

No, she decided, walking was definitely the better idea. She scrambled up the embankment after him.

"We can stop by the sheriff's office," Cassie said as she fell into step beside him.

"No," Dan retorted flatly. Ed had introduced him to the sheriff on an earlier visit, and the man was no match for an assassin hired by the mob. What he needed to do was get in touch with Harry and have him notify the Justice Department. They would know the best way to protect Cassie.

Cassie stopped dead in the road and stared at him in dumbfounded disbelief. His jaws were tightly clenched, making the muscles cord beneath the skin. The lines in his cheeks were deep slashes of tension, and his eyes ... Cassie wanted to weep at the bleakness of his expression. It was as if he'd lost his last friend and didn't know what to do about it. She wanted to fling her arms around him and protect him. But how could she protect him when she didn't know who the enemy was?

"Why not?" she demanded.

"What would you tell him?"

"A few facts would be nice," she shot back. "Of course, that presupposes that I know any. Which I don't. You wouldn't care to enlighten me, would you?"

"The brake line ruptured," he suggested, not wanting to confirm her conclusion and add to her fears. "Brake lines do that occasionally. Even in new cars."

"And men lie!" Cassie bit out. "That happens far more than occasionally." Furious at his refusal to trust her enough to explain what was going on, she turned and stalked up the road.

Dan watched the stiff line of her body as a feeling of utter hopelessness seeped through him. He felt as if his whole world was in the process of tumbling down about his ears and he didn't know how to prop it back up. It now seemed obvious that the poisoned coffee wasn't just a boyish prank gone awry. Any more than what had just happened with the car's brakes had been an accident. He'd felt the smooth cut in the brake line. It had been sliced with something very sharp—in an attempt to kill him. And the killer had almost snared Cassie in his deadly trap.

His guts twisted painfully at the thought of Cassie dead, of the laughter in her eyes forever extinguished. And what would she have died for? he thought wearily. For nothing. For nothing more important than to assuage the injured pride of some two-bit hood who thought he was the reincarnation of Al Capone.

An overwhelming tiredness seemed to weigh down on him, pushing him into the pavement. His whole life seemed so futile. He'd been writing exposés on corruption and hate and crime for almost twenty years and what did he have to show for it?

A minor-league gangster had almost succeeded in killing the most important thing in the world to him. He stared at Cassie's rigid back as she stalked on, a few steps ahead of him as if she couldn't bear to look at him. He sighed despondently. He didn't blame her. He wanted to give her everything, and what he was likely to do was get her killed. And if that happened... He swallowed against the rising fear that clogged the back of his throat.

It couldn't. Whatever else happened, he had to protect Cassie... because he loved her. The undeniable truth partially thawed the frozen feeling of fear that gripped him. He loved her. He repeated the words to himself like a talisman. He loved her bright mind and her sexy body and her kindness and the way she was willing to inconvenience herself for her elderly aunt. He loved everything about her, even the way she tilted her head to one side when she was thinking about something.

He shivered as the warmth of his feelings slowly seeped away, leaving a cold reality in their wake. He might love Cassie, but what good was that to her? Association with him was a one-way ticket to the morgue.

He had to leave China View; abruptly, he faced the unwelcome fact. Cassie would be safe only if he were gone. Damn his job! he thought with sudden ferocity. The only way she would be permanently safe would be if he weren't writing the kinds of articles that made him a moving target. He needed to resign from his job now. Not at some time in the future when he'd found something else to take its place, but right now.

Then, when Buczek was no longer a threat, he would look around and find something else to do. Maybe he ought to try writing editorials for worthy causes like school bond issues, he thought ruefully. He certainly hadn't had much luck convincing people to stop killing each other. Maybe he should concentrate on trying to get them to make smaller changes closer to home. Things like buying computers for kids and improving local housing conditions for the poor or setting up senior-citizen centers. Who was to say that in the long run those things might not be as important as what he'd tried to do?

Dan watched the way the brisk wind off the sea whipped Cassie's bright hair around her head, trapping minute particles of glowing color in its strands. The glimmering prisms of light made her look like an angel. Pain lanced through him. If she associated with him much longer, she might really get to be an angel. A resurgence of panicky fear filled him. He had to leave. Immediately. He would wait until Justin returned to the inn, call him from Ed's office and ask him to drive into town and pick him up.

If he left now, there would be no reason to worry Cassie with the sordid facts. No reason for her to have to know that he had a hit man after him. And since he intended to resign from his job, it would never happen again, he rationalized.

But if he didn't tell her what this was all about, then what kind of relationship would they have? The question gnawed uncomfortably at him. One of the things he liked best about Cassie was her truthful, forthright manner. Surely she deserved the truth in return? But if he told her the truth, she might well decide that he was not a safe man to know. A numbing sensation crept through him, adding a leaden weight to his limbs and making it hard for him to keep up with her furious pace.

He had to tell her. Cassie Whitney was the most important thing that had ever happened to him. She held out hope for a meaningful future, but he couldn't hold on to that hope with lies. Even lies of omission. It would change their relationship, irrevocably tarnish it. Unconsciously he squared his shoulders. He had to risk telling her. And if she decided that he shouldn't come back when this was all over... His mind refused to even consider the possibility.

"Cas—" His voice broke with the effort he was exerting to sound normal. "Cassie?"

She glanced over her shoulder at him, automatically checking his leg despite her anger.

"I—" He broke off once more, shoving shaking fingers through his disheveled hair.

Cassie stopped and waited for him to catch up with her, her anger dissipating in the face of his obvious agitation. She studied his tense features. He looked... haunted.

"You were right," he finally blurted out.

"About what?" she asked cautiously, hoping he was finally going to trust her enough to tell her the truth, but fearing that this might be yet one more subterfuge.

"About them not being accidents. I think they're the work of a hit man."

Cassie stared at him in dumbfounded shock. She wasn't exactly sure what she'd expected him to say, but a hit man hadn't been among the possibilities.

"But professional killers are efficient," she objected. "Or did the person you made mad enough to hire this inept killer not have enough money to buy the real thing?"

"Buczek has plenty of money."

"Buczek?" Cassie frowned as the name triggered a faint memory. "Wasn't he involved in some kind of graft with one of the municipal unions in New York City?"

"Among other things."

Cassie stared into Dan's brown eyes. His honest brown eyes. She would never, ever believe that he was an associate of a gangster. Which mean that he had to be an opponent.

"What did you do to him?" she asked.

Dan shrugged. "Telling the truth may set you free, but it can also set you up as a target. I wrote a series of articles that made it impossible for the authorities to continue to pretend that Buczek was just a well-intentioned union boss with an abrasive manner. Single-handedly, I managed to get the Justice Department involved."

"No, you didn't. I remember those articles. They were written by Leland Trav..." Her voice trailed away into silence as she stared at him in sudden comprehension. Leland Travis, internationally acclaimed reporter, and *her* Dan Travis were one and the same. She'd been reading his articles most of her adult life. She'd simply never seen a picture of him.

Cassie shook her head, trying to dislodge the idea. It wouldn't budge.

"Say something," he demanded, tension making his voice harsh.

Cassie gestured impotently. "I'm not sure what to say."

"I'm sorry. I never meant to involve you. And for what it's worth, I really thought Brett had poisoned the coffee after we found his slingshot in the shed. Even now..." He grimaced. "Poison and cut brake lines simply aren't part of a hit man's normal MO "

"Was that what happened to your leg and arm?" Cassie asked.

"No," he muttered. "That happened in Bosnia while I was riding in a Red Cross hospital truck." He snorted. "I was in New York to recuperate. I think this time I'll try to lose myself somewhere safer, like East St. Louis or Washington, D.C."

"You aren't going anywhere." Cassie immediately vetoed the idea. Whoever was in charge of helping him stay alive was doing an abysmal job. If she let Dan leave China View, he would probably get blown away before he even reached the anonymity of a big city.

"I'm not?" Dan felt the tightness around his chest ease fractionally at her determined expression. He didn't want to go, he admitted. Even though he knew that he should, for his own sake as well as Cassie's, he still wanted to stay close to her for as long as he could. To bask in the warmth of her smile. To lose himself in the wonder of her lovemaking.

"Absolutely not!" she said emphatically. "We'll neutralize this hit man ourselves."

And then what? The question popped into her mind. Loving Dan Travis, inept insurance salesman, was one thing. Loving Leland Travis, world-renowned reporter, was quite another.

Worry about one thing at a time, she told herself. Her most pressing concern at the moment was trying to keep the man himself alive.

# Nine

"It's Smith" Cassie announced.

"Where?" Dan glanced around the outskirts of Levington, which they'd finally reached.

"Not here."

"Too bad," Dan muttered. "A lift would have been nice."

"Don't you see?" she said impatiently. "Smith has to be the hit man."

"No, I don't see. Smith may be a royal pain in the ass, but he isn't a killer."

"Then who's your candidate? Functioning as a hired assassin is beyond Brett. At the moment," she added darkly. "And it must be someone staying at the inn."

"Not necessarily. The car was parked outside. After dark, anyone could have sabotaged it. They could be staying anywhere in the area."

"Yeah, but what about the cyanide in the sugar bowl? We would have noticed a stranger hanging around."

"They could be two separate incidents," Dan said slowly. "Brett really could have done that."

"Possibly," Cassie conceded, reluctant to give up her prime suspect.

"Besides, Smith works at the paper with me and his name is really Sloan," Dan added. "Harry, our editor, sent him to keep an eye on things."

"So I can add incompetence to the list of reasons I don't like him," Cassie said with a sniff.

"I didn't believe there was any danger at China View, either. And neither did Harry." Dan tried to be fair.

"There won't be for long," Cassie vowed. "No hit man is a match for a truly determined woman. We'll nail the bastard!"

Dan felt a curious melting sensation nibble at the tension gripping him, as if a weight were being lifted off him. It didn't make a great deal of sense. The hit man was still loose and still after him, but just sharing his worries with Cassie had made him feel better.

"But if it isn't Smith, then who is it?" Cassie continued her line of thinking as they crossed the street and headed toward the newspaper office.

Dan shrugged. "Beats me. It can't be Byron Essel. No assassin in his right mind would bring his family along on a hit. Especially not when it includes a highly memorable kid like Brett."

"True," Cassie conceded. "And unless her chosen weapon is talking her victim to death, we can rule out Madam Rowinski. Gertie's been cleaning guest rooms at the inn for Aunt Hannah for almost five years now. And while the man who does the gardens drinks a little too much—actually a lot too much," she amended honestly, "he was born here in the village, and except for a stint in the navy during the Second World War, has never left."

"What about your ghost?" Dan asked thoughtfully.

"Jonas? Aunt Hannah called the local casting director of the village's amateur theater and asked her to find someone to play the part, and she sent him along. Besides, we decided to hire a ghost before you came."

Cassie heaved a frustrated sigh as they reached the newspaper office. "Which leaves us right where we started. Nowhere."

"Not entirely. We know someone really is after me." He held the door open for her and then followed her inside.

Cassie glanced around the deserted office. "Anybody here?"

Ed furtively stuck his head around the stockroom door at the back. "Oh, it's just you two."

"Who were you expecting?" Cassie asked curiously as the editor crossed the room, tipped up a slat of the venetian blind and peered out into the street.

"Martha from over at the full-figure dress shop." Ed grimaced. "The blamed woman doesn't like the copy I wrote for her ad. She wants a refund. Dammit, I don't know what she expects. I'm a newspaperman, not some—"

"Ahem." Cassie looked down her nose at him. "Before you put your foot in your mouth, remember that some of us take pride in writing ad copy."

"You wouldn't write it for me, would you?" A crafty look tightened Ed's features.

"No," Cassie said succinctly. "Unlike Dan here, I'm not susceptible to blackmail."

"Blackmail? Me?" Ed looked the picture of outraged innocence.

"Stow it, Ed." Dan sank down on a chair and began to absently rub his aching thigh. "Cassie knows."

"Oh." The man looked crestfallen. "Does that mean you won't finish the editorial?"

"No." Dan pulled a folded sheet of paper out of his back pocket and handed it to him.

"Thanks." Ed beamed at him. "Anything I can do for you?"

"You can give us a lift back to the inn," Cassie said with a worried look at Dan's leg.

Ed stared at them in surprise. "Don't tell me you walked to town?"

"No. Our car's brakes failed on the cliff road about a mile back," Dan said with a warning glance at Cassie. He didn't need Ed trying to get a story out of this.

"The cliffs! You're damn lucky to be in one piece if your brakes gave out up there. Here. You need a drink." Ed reached into his bottom desk drawer and pulled out a bottle of Scotch. "Cassie, would you get some of those paper cups from the watercooler?"

Cassie got them. She wasn't normally in favor of responding to an emergency with alcohol, but in this case she was willing to make an exception. Dan needed something to numb the pain he was obviously feeling in his leg.

Ed poured them each a cup and then lifted his own. "To life, long may it last."

"To life," Dan echoed somberly and took a hefty swallow.

"To life," Cassie repeated with grim determination.

Ed quickly finished his drink and refilled his cup. "Don't look at me like that, girl!" he ordered as he noticed Cassie's raised eyebrows. "You're beginning to sound like my wife."

"I didn't say a word," she protested. "Besides, if you're driving us to the inn, it certainly is my business."

"True." He regretfully poured his drink back into the bottle.

"It's just that I'm a bit down. You see, my daughter in Florida finally had her baby. A ten-pound, seven-ounce girl." Ed brightened momentarily. "And my wife flew out this morning to be with her, but I can't leave the newspaper." His face fell. "I'm ready to admit that the time has finally come to sell the paper. If the truth were known, it's getting to be too much for me to handle. The problem's going to be finding a buyer."

"Why would that be a problem?" Dan asked.

Ed sighed. "Because the paper doesn't make a living for a family. If it weren't for the income my wife has from her parents' estate, I'd have had to give up years ago."

*He* had an outside source of income, Dan thought as he slowly sipped his drink. He wouldn't need to worry about how much income the paper generated. Even if it lost money, he could take it as a tax write-off.

He glanced around the dusty office with an assessing eye. It needed work. A little remodeling. Some paint. And he already knew the printing press was on its last leg. His gaze lingered on the empty desk under the window. He could almost see Cassie sitting there, creating innovative copy for the full-figured dress shop. But would she want to? Doubts crept in. She was carving out a very impressive career for herself in New York. Would she want to trade it for life in rural New Hampshire? With him? An uprush of longing constricted his breathing. It would be so perfect. He and Cassie could run Ed's paper and crusade for local causes.

But first he had to survive his last crusade. Reality brought him up short. First he had to neutralize Buczek and his hit man, then he could risk finding out just how deeply Cassie's feelings for him went.

"Drat!" Cassie muttered as she spilled some whiskey on the front of her yellow silk blouse. She brushed ineffectively at the spot and then got to her feet. "I'll be back in a moment. I want to try to sponge this off before it stains."

Dan waited until she'd disappeared into the washroom and then hurriedly turned to Ed. "I'll give you ten thousand dollars for a ninety-day option to buy the paper," he said.

Ed's eyes widened in surprise. "You! Buy this paper? Why?" he asked bluntly. "There isn't a paper in the country that wouldn't kill to have you on its staff."

Dan winced at Ed's choice of expression. "I'm tired." He gave him part of the truth. "Tired of all the graft, murder and mayhem a big city paper covers. I want to get away from it all."

"Well," Ed said slowly, "it doesn't get much 'awayer' than Levington. But if that's the way you feel, why just an option? Why not an offer?"

Dan instinctively glanced toward the washroom. His feelings for Cassie were too new and far too personal for him to risk exposing them to Ed's view.

Ed followed his gaze and a knowing expression lighted his face. "Oh, ho! Like that, is it?"

"I haven't said anything to her yet." Dan hurriedly tried to head the newsman off. "There are complications."

"Well, I hope you work them out," Ed said sincerely. "The paper needs some fresh young blood like yours."

If the hit man had his way, his fresh young blood was going to be spread all over the village, Dan thought grimly.

"As for that option—" Ed rubbed his jaw thoughtfully "—keep your money. I'll give you first refusal for the next three months."

The editor held out his hand, and Dan shook it, feeling that in spite of the problems with Buczek, his life was finally beginning to turn around, to take the direction he'd unconsciously been seeking for years. Now all he had to do was unmask the assassin and convince Cassie that she loved him one-tenth as much as he loved her. What he didn't know was how was he supposed to accomplish either task.

But though he worried about it the entire ride home, Dan was no closer to a solution by the time Ed deposited them in front of the inn almost an hour later.

"I think I'll go upstairs and call Harry. Ask him to run a background check on our fellow guests," Dan said as he followed Cassie into the inn. "He can also notify the Justice Department and see what they recommend. In the meantime I don't think we'll be in any danger if we stay inside. Both attacks have come while we were away from China View."

"I think you're right," Cassie agreed. "And make sure you ask this Harry of yours to check up on Smith, too. I'll get you the home addresses of our guests."

She stuck her head into the sun-room, but the only person there was Madam Rowinski. The woman was sitting by the window with her eyes closed. For one awful moment Cassie thought she was dead, but then she gave a snuffle, followed by a snort, and shifted slightly.

Quietly, Cassie backed out of the room and, motioning for Dan to follow her, headed toward the front desk. She grimaced as she opened the reservation book and began to copy out addresses.

"This whole thing has me so spooked I'm beginning to see bodies everywhere," she muttered, handing Dan the list.

He glanced down at it. "I'll call Harry right away."

"I'll be in the kitchen when you're through. Come and tell me what he said."

Dan grasped the back of her neck and gently pulled her toward him. He lowered his head and whispered against her lips, "I'll tell you anything."

"I'll settle for the truth," she murmured. The warmth of his breath fanned her skin, heightening her awareness of him. She reached up and ran the tip of her finger around his outer ear, smiling to herself at the shudder that shook his frame. His mouth covered hers hungrily.

Cassie allowed herself the momentary luxury of reveling in the melting sensation his mobile lips produced in her. Then she reluctantly stepped back. Opening her eyelids, which felt weighted with desire, she stared up into his gleaming eyes.

"Go call your editor," she finally said. "We shouldn't be indulging in . . ."

"Lovemaking?" he suggested with a boyishly hopeful look that made her heart quiver.

"We should be so lucky," she muttered. "Assassins first. Lovemaking second."

"Assassins first," Dan reluctantly agreed, feeling as if his whole life were on hold. "And you be careful while I'm upstairs."

"I won't go near anyone strange, and I won't leave the inn," Cassie promised, meaning every word.

She watched Dan until he'd disappeared up the stairs and then hurried into the kitchen. It was probably too early for her aunt to be back, but Jonas might be around. She found him sitting at the kitchen table, drinking a cup of coffee and eating cookies.

"Jonas, I need you to do something for me."

"If'n I can," he agreed promptly.

"Well..." Cassie paused, uncertain of exactly how much to tell him. Everything, she finally decided. If she was *asking* him to watch out for a killer, he had to know enough to make sure he didn't get hurt himself.

"Someone is trying to kill Dan," she said baldly.

Jonas' bushy black eyebrows shot up in surprise. "Here? In my house?" He seemed more angered at where they were doing it than the fact that they were doing it in the first place.

"In the area," Cassie said soothingly. "This morning someone sabotaged his car so it crashed on the cliffs, which makes us think that the poisoned coffee from yesterday wasn't Brett after all."

"Who is this villain?" Jonas seemed to swell with outrage. "I'll rip him limb from limb." He suddenly paled, and shot a quick glance up at the ceiling. "I mean, I'll make him see the error of his ways."

"No one can overhear us," Cassie assured him. "We checked the front of the inn before I came in. Except for Madam Rowinski, who's asleep, it's deserted. We're safe."

"That's what you think, gal," Jonas muttered.

"Anyway, I can't tell you because I don't know," Cassie continued. "We're sure it's a hit man."

Jonas frowned. "Hit man?"

"Hired assassin. What I'd like you to do is to keep an eye on Smith."

"You think it's him?" Jonas asked skeptically.

Cassie grimaced. "I don't trust him, but Dan says it can't be him. That Smith works at the same newspaper."

Jonas slowly stroked his beard. "Men can be bought," he finally said.

"True," Cassie agreed. "And from the looks of his wardrobe, Justin Smith is a man with very expensive tastes."

"I'll keep an eye on him. If'n he's your assassin, why, that might be an even better good deed." Jonas' eyes lit up.

"Than what?" Cassie asked in confusion.

He hurriedly got to his feet. "Never you mind. I'll take care of it." With an encouraging smile, he headed out the back door.

Cassie absently picked up Jonas' dirty dishes and stuffed them in the dishwasher as she tried to plan. But she couldn't seem to get beyond the fact that someone was trying to kill Dan. It all seemed so surrealistic.

She jumped as the hallway door squeaked slightly. It swung open to reveal the object of her thoughts.

"Did you get hold of your editor?" she asked.

"No. His secretary said he got a call about some killing or other and rushed out of the office, saying he'd be back shortly. I asked her to have him call me the minute he does."

"Did you see Smith while you were upstairs?" she demanded.

"Yes, and he was just as horrified as we were."

Cassie grimaced. "Maybe. Or maybe he's just a good actor. So what do we do now?"

Dan's eyes began to glow with sudden enthusiasm. "I have an idea." His mouth swooped without warning to cover her lips, and Cassie felt her own sense of excitement burgeoning. She snuggled against him, her arms going around his waist to pull him even closer. She could feel the heavy twist of the cotton yarn of his sweater and the underlying warmth of his skin. Slipping her hands beneath his sweater, she pressed her palms against his taut flesh. A soft sigh escaped her at the pleasurable feel. Mindlessly, she rubbed her hands across his back, reveling in the sensation.

Touching him felt so right. So normal. As if she had been waiting her whole life for this man. She wanted to go on touching him forever. A sudden chill sliced through her sense of euphoria as she remembered that it wasn't her whole life that was the problem. It was his. And his life might be very short if the hit man managed to have his way.

"We need to plan," she muttered as she moved away.

"Instinct works much better." Dan tried to pull her back into his arms.

"This is no time for lovemaking," she chided him. "First we have to figure out how to keep you alive, and then we can enjoy the results."

Dan sighed. Walking over to the counter, he poured himself a cup of coffee and sat down at the table. He took a hefty swallow, winced at the bitter taste, reached for the sugar bowl and then seemed to think better of it.

"It's safe," Cassie assured him. "I locked up all the poisons yesterday. Besides, Jonas had some in his coffee. What do you think we should do until we hear from your editor?"

"Smith's going to keep an eye on my room upstairs. If anyone goes near it, he'll see them. Other than that, what can we do?"

"Deduct. What was it Sherlock Holmes said? First you eliminate the impossible. What remains is the answer, no matter how improbable."

"Or imponderable," Dan said dryly. "We've already been over this. And the only conclusion we can draw is that in all probability the assassin isn't staying here at the inn."

"I'll bet he's staying over at the resort. They don't care who they let in."

Dan grinned at her aggrieved expression.

"Ah, there you are, my dear, Mr. Travis."

Cassie jumped as her aunt seemed to materialize at the back door. "I didn't see Mr. Travis' car as I drove up and I was afraid that you might not have gotten back yet."

"The brakes weren't working quite right, so we left it in town. Ed Veach gave us a lift back," Cassie improvised, seeing no reason to burden her aunt with the fact that one of their guests had been marked for death. Hannah already had enough to worry about.

"Very wise. That cliff road is dangerous in the normal way, and if your brakes should fail..." The elderly woman shook her head in disapproval at the idea of the resulting chaos.

"I only came back to pick up some papers, dear," she went on. "We've asked the judge to grant us an injunction to stop that developer from demolishing the apartment building, and the hearing is slated for late this afternoon. I promised Jessie I'd help her present their side of the issue, so I'm not sure exactly when I'll be back. If the weather forecast I just heard about a thunderstorm turns out to be accurate, I may simply stay in town until the worst of it is over."

"Not to worry," Cassie assured her. "I can handle dinner."

Hannah kissed her cheek. "Thank you, dear. I'll be back as soon as I can."

Thoughtfully, Dan watched Hannah hurry out. "You're very lucky to have her," he told Cassie.

"Yes, she's a darling. But we still haven't decided what we're going to do."

"That's because there isn't anything we can do. Other than wait to see if Harry turns up anything on the inn's guests."

"You can also play least-in-sight," Cassie suggested.

"I *could* hide in your bedroom." Dan gave her a wicked grin that made her heart thump with excitement. What was the matter with her? she chided herself. How could she be thinking about making love to him when there was so much danger swirling about them? The problem was that when she was with him, nothing else mattered, she conceded. Hit men lurking in closets simply became an annoyance.

"Be serious," she ordered.

"It doesn't get any more serious than making love to you." There was a strange note in Dan's voice that sent a tremor of hope through her, but she refused to examine his words for any deeper meanings. It wasn't the time, she told herself.

"I asked Jonas to keep an eye on Smith, so if he makes a move, we'll know. And in the meantime I think we ought to stay in the kitchen."

"It's four o'clock." Dan checked his watch. "How long are we going to hide?"

"As long as it takes." She opened the refrigerator and peered inside. "We might as well start dinner."

"I'll help," Dan offered.

They had finished making the main course as well as a batch of Jonas' favorite raspberry tarts for dessert and were washing up when the Essels called from a small town thirty miles west of the inn to say that they were in the midst of a violent thunderstorm and would not be returning for dinner as they'd planned. Instead, they were going to wait for it to blow itself out.

"Which means that the storm should reach us very shortly," Cassie said.

Dan frowned. "Personally, I'd rather have the brat than a storm. The way things are going, the inn'll probably get struck by lightning."

"It hasn't yet, and we have a generator to run the lights if the electricity fails," Cassie said in satisfaction. "Besides, if it's storming out, the hit man isn't going to try anything. It'd be too risky, to say nothing of too uncomfortable. Not only that but the only people we have to feed now are Madam Rowinski and your Mr. Smith."

"They won't be much trouble," Dan said.

He was only partially right. Smith was no trouble at all. He elected to have his dinner on a tray in his room, saying that from there he could watch both Dan's room and the road leading into the inn.

Madam Rowinski, on the other hand, proved to be an infinite amount of trouble. She kept up a running monologue throughout dinner, until Cassie's ears rang with the continual babble and Dan finally retreated to his room under the pretext of needing to make a phone call.

Cassie's deliverance came in the form of the first ominous rumbles of thunder in the distance. Madam Rowinski gasped and told Cassie that storms always gave her a migraine. She intended to take a sleeping pill and go to bed before it struck, she announced. And could she please have a glass of warm milk to take with her and perhaps just a few cookies and one or two of the raspberry tarts from dinner?

Cassie, who would have been willing to turn over the entire contents of the pantry to get rid of her, hurried out to the kitchen to put milk in the microwave oven. To her infinite relief, Madam Rowinski, after spending another fifteen minutes detailing just how delicate her nerves were, finally went up to her room.

Afraid that she might return, Cassie scurried out to the kitchen to hide.

Dan found her there forty minutes later. "Is she gone?" he asked with a furtive glance around.

"But not forgotten," Cassie said wryly. "I swear her poor husband was probably talked to death."

"She—" Dan winced as a crack of thunder sounded overhead.

Cassie pulled aside the kitchen curtain and peered into the darkness. "It's getting closer," she reported, stating the obvious.

"It's too bad your ghost gave up his cover," Dan said. "This sounds like his kind of weather."

"I'd rather have a vampire than a ghost any day." Cassie purposefully tried to lighten the oppressive atmosphere. "Vampires are romantic."

He looked at her in disbelief, and then a mischievous expression warmed his eyes. He slowly approached her.

"If I remember my Dracula movies, he would capture the girl like this...." Dan drew her against him. His warm body pressed against hers from shoulder to thigh, wreaking havoc with her thought processes. She swallowed at the convulsive dryness in her throat and peered up into his face, her eyes lingering on the enticing tilt of his firm lips. She studied their dusky pinkness, remembering the enticing feel and the intoxicating taste of them against her mouth.

"Then—" Dan's voice deepened to a husky murmur "—he would pounce." He began to nibble on the vein pulsating in the side of her neck. "Ah, my *sveet,* I *vill* make you mine," he murmured in a fractured accent, but Cassie didn't even notice. Her whole concentration was on the exhilerating touch of his warm lips. On the exciting feel of his faintly scratchy chin as it rubbed across her skin.

"Mmm." She arched her body against him, shivering slightly as her breasts were crushed into his chest. Her worries were slowly seeping away, leaving in their wake only a delight in his touch. "Now I know why Dracula was so successful with women," she muttered, twisting closer.

"You haven't seen anything yet," Dan vowed. "They couldn't show the good part on television."

Cassie giggled happily. "I beg to differ with you, but there isn't anything they don't show on television. They—"

"Good Lord!" Dan's arms tightened convulsively as a particularly violent bolt of lightning briefly illuminated the night sky. It was immediately followed by utter darkness and a deadening rumble of thunder.

"The lights just went." He announced the obvious.

"Yup." Cassie nibbled on his earlobe.

"Shouldn't we do something about it?"

"Send a letter of complaint to God about the way he's arranging the weather?" She trailed the tips of her fingers over his cheek, smiling slightly as he shuddered beneath her exploration.

"I was thinking of something a little more practical. Smith won't be able to see anything in the dark."

"I suppose we should," Cassie conceded, reluctant to move out of his arms. "If those pills of Madam Rowinski haven't already put her to sleep, she's probably frightened out of her wits."

"The woman doesn't have any wits to be frightened out of," Dan said dryly. "But I will admit I certainly don't want to spend what's left of our evening listening to her talk."

"And talk and talk." Cassie sighed. "I swear I've never met anyone who could use so many words to say so little."

"So how do we fix the lights?" Dan asked.

"We just flip on the generator. This happens all the time during storms. The electric company is pretty good about restoring service within the hour."

"Where is this generator?" Dan let her go with a reluctance that warmed her heart.

"In the storage shed in the back of the garden." Cassie fumbled around in a drawer and finally located a flashlight by touch. She switched it on and headed out the door with Dan right behind her.

She shivered convulsively as a gust of wind-driven rain lashed against her body. She quickened her pace.

"Slow down. It's dark out here." Dan focused on the thin pool of light the flashlight made on the brick pathway.

Cassie cast a nervous glance around the darkness, which was filled with shapes and objects that seemed to threaten. Don't let your imagination run away with you, she ordered herself as she lifted the latch on the shed and pushed the door open.

"Now I know what stygian darkness means," Dan said as the flashlight cut a weak path through the darkness.

Cassie breathed a sigh of relief when a quick sweep of the small shed revealed it to be empty. She hadn't expected to find anybody lurking out here, not really. But somehow the storm, on top of the day's events, made her imagination susceptible to all kinds of irrational fears.

She handed the flashlight to Dan and said, "Focus the light on the front of the generator." She pulled her now-damp sweater a little closer to her chilled body and squatted down beside the machine. As she had often done in the past, she opened the valve on the gas tank and pushed the start-up switch. To her relief, the engine immediately purred to efficient life.

"There." She looked up at him. "The way things have been going, I was half expecting it not to work."

"Oh, *it* works."

Cassie looked up at the strange note in Dan's voice. "What's the matter?" she asked, trying to read his expression in the reflected light from the flashlight he was holding. It was impossible.

"Look." He gestured with the flashlight, back toward the house.

# Ten

---

**P**uzzled, Cassie slowly got to her feet and moved around him to the door of the shed. She stared uncomprehendingly at the inn. It was still shrouded in darkness. Complete, total darkness. She turned and looked at the generator. It was clearly running.

"So why aren't the lights on?" she asked in confusion. "It always worked before."

"Could that last bolt of lightning have hit something and tripped the circuit breakers?" Dan suggested, wanting desperately to believe the answer was as harmless as that even though common sense told him this was simply one coincidence too many.

"Maybe. It is possible," she said more strongly, trying to convince herself.

"Where are the circuit breakers?" Dan asked.

"In the basement."

"No way are we going down into a dark basement," Dan said flatly. "I don't like this." He stared across the garden at the dark bulk of the inn. "I don't like this at all."

Cassie sighed. "I can't say I'm real keen on it, either, but it really could just be the circuit breakers."

"And it could be the hit man making his move." Dan switched off the flashlight.

Cassie blinked, trying to adjust her vision to the sudden darkness. "Why'd you do that?"

"There's no sense advertising where we are to anyone waiting out there. You stay here and I'll—"

"No!" Cassie emphatically vetoed the idea. There was no way she was about to allow him to face whatever was out there on his own. Who knew what might happen if she weren't there to protect him. Why, he didn't even have enough sense to suspect Smith.

"We can't stay here," he said. "If it really is a hit man, trapping us in here would be child's play."

"You aren't going out there by yourself."

"Cassie, be reasonable. It's me he wants to..."

"Kill," she said starkly. "And I won't let him. If you try to leave me here, I'll follow you."

She would, too, and then he wouldn't know if the bumps in the night behind him were Cassie or the hit man. And he wanted her along, he admitted. He knew he should be brave and fearless and go face whatever it was out there by himself, but he wanted Cassie with him. He was so tired of facing things by himself.

"All right, you can come," he said, giving in. "But stay behind me."

"Right behind you." She pressed up against him.

Dan gulped as the desire to turn and kiss her momentarily overrode his other worries. "Not that close," he said. "You're distracting me."

Cassie obediently inched back slightly. "I think," she said slowly, "the time has come to forget about your editor and the Justice Department and call the sheriff."

"Yes," Dan conceded. "I wouldn't have waited this long for Harry to call back if I hadn't thought we'd be safe inside."

"We don't know that we won't be. If this really is the work of the hit man, it could be because he wants to drive us from the safety of the inn. Let's go find out." She felt a curious mixture of anticipation and dread wash through her. Even though she was afraid of what might be out there, she still wanted to face it, to defeat it so that she could get on with her life.

"Stay behind me," Dan repeated as he silently slipped through the shed door. Keeping to the deep shadows at the edge of the pathway, he cautiously made his way toward the inn, with Cassie one step behind him. To his vague surprise, nothing happened. There were no flashes of light at any of the windows. No one took a shot at them. There was nothing out of the ordinary.

"So far, so good," Dan whispered as they reached the back porch. They opened the kitchen door and paused, straining to hear something. Anything. It was silent as a tomb.

Their intense concentration was broken when a huge bolt of lightning cracked directly overhead. Cassie inadvertently squeaked in surprise. The sharply acrid smell of ozone filled the air, and she instinctively pressed against the comforting warmth of Dan's body.

"Inside." He yanked her into the kitchen as the rain began to pour down in earnest.

"Let's look out the front window and see if there's a strange car in the parking lot," Cassie whispered. She started to slip around him, but he grabbed her arm.

"I know where everything is," she insisted. "You don't. You'll be bumping into things in the dark, and if there really is someone lurking about, they'll know right where we are."

"True," Dan reluctantly conceded. "Just be careful." He followed her as she silently crept through the kitchen and into the hallway.

Cassie desperately concentrated, trying to hear sounds that shouldn't be there, but she couldn't. If there were any unusual noises, they were being drowned out by the hammering of the rain against the inn's slate roof.

When they reached the lobby window, Cassie peered out into the darkness. "Hannibal and his whole herd of elephants could be camped out there for all we can see," she muttered in frustration.

"Wait a minute." Dan's soft breath lifted the hair around her ear.

She realized what he meant a second later when another bolt of lightning illuminated the parking lot with the brilliance of daytime. They had a clear view of two cars—Smith's and Madam Rowinski's.

"No visitors," Dan muttered.

"Unless they left their car on the road and hiked up here, which isn't any too likely in this weather," Cassie whispered. "Besides, if they'd never been at the inn, how would they know where the circuit-breaker box was so they could sabotage the lights?"

Her analysis made sense, Dan conceded. Either the power being out was the result of the storm or the assassin was already in residence. But as for her insistence that Smith was responsible . . . Dan frowned. He just couldn't buy Sloan as the villain of the piece. It was too unlikely.

"Did you actually see the Essels leave the inn?" Dan was very careful to keep his voice down.

"No, Aunt Hannah said they'd gone. But I did take their call earlier this evening when they said they wouldn't be back for dinner."

"Who did you talk to?" Dan asked.

"Mrs. Essel. You think she took Brett out to establish an alibi while her husband snuck back to...?" Cassie scooted closer to Dan.

"Or never left."

"The sooner we get some help the better," Cassie muttered. "Come on." She crept toward the reception desk and, hunching down behind it, pulled the receiver off the hook.

"What's the matter?" Dan asked at her sudden stillness.

"It's dead." She swallowed uneasily. "Phones have a built-in power source from batteries. They aren't affected by power outages."

"So we can ditch the storm theory. Someone all too human sabotaged the lights and the phone."

"Do you have a weapon?"

His sigh echoed through the air, seeming to catch on the tendrils of darkness. "A gun," he said tiredly.

"Good, we'll—"

"Locked in the trunk of the rental car. I put it there when I thought Brett was dabbling in poison. I was afraid he might get his hands on it and kill himself. Or one of us. And it's still there, because the crash jammed the trunk."

"So it did. If I were the superstitious sort, I'd be worried. Fate does not seem to be on our side." Cassie took a deep breath. "Well, we can't leave Madam Rowinski behind and make a run for it. The hit man might think she was faking sleep and waste her just to make sure. And then there's the very real possibility that Aunt Hannah could return while we were gone and walk right in on the killer." Cassie gulped. "She wouldn't stand a chance."

"Maybe Smith brought a weapon," Dan said thoughtfully.

"He might have," Cassie agreed. "Of course, if he's the hit man, we can take that as a fact. But where is he? Madam Rowinski is obviously still out from the sleeping pill, but Smith..."

Dan glanced up toward the black space where he knew the stairwell was. "A good point. If the lights went out, wouldn't a person normally come down to see what the problem was?" He felt a tremor of uncertainty lift the hairs on his arms. Had Cassie been right all along? Was it Smith?

"I'm liking this whole situation less by the second," she muttered. "Let's go into the kitchen, get a couple of Aunt Hannah's biggest knives and sneak up the back stairs and surprise Smith."

"Let's surprise whoever it is," Dan corrected her. "Keeping an open mind to danger goes a long way to keeping one alive."

"You keep an open mind, and I'll concentrate on Smith." Cassie started inching her way back toward the kitchen. No one disputed their passage. They were able to find a hefty meat cleaver and a wicked-looking boning knife with a razor-sharp edge.

Feeling slightly better now that they had some means of protecting themselves, Cassie silently led the way up the back stairs. She crouched at the top of the stairwell, waiting until a bolt of lightning illuminated the hallway. It was empty.

She jerked around and gave Dan a quick kiss, catching him by surprise. She didn't know what was about to happen, but she did know that whatever it was, it would be more bearable with the memory of his kiss on her lips.

Careful to keep her back to the wall so that they couldn't be surprised from behind, Cassie flittered down the hallway like a shadow. Past Madam Rowinski's closed door, past Dan's room to stop in front of Smith's. Sending up a silent prayer for help, she reached out for the knob, freezing when she realized that the door was slightly ajar. Groping behind her, she grasped Dan's hand and put it on the door so that he'd know, too.

He inched around her and, crouching down, waited for another roll of thunder to cover the sound of his entry.

When it came, he shoved open the door. His gaze hastily swept the room. There was nothing to see. It appeared to be empty, which made no sense. Creeping inside, he leaned back against the wall to the right of the door. If Smith wasn't in his room, where was he? Not downstairs or they'd have seen him. And he couldn't have left the inn, because his car was still here.

Dan stealthily moved farther into the room, with Cassie right on his heels. She made a good conspirator, he thought with a flash of pride. She had more guts than most men carrying an Uzi.

He stopped at the foot of Smith's bed and held his breath, trying to listen for the sound of someone else breathing, but the pounding rain drowned out such an elusive noise. Finally, he decided to risk using the flashlight to search Smith's things for a gun or, at the very least, for a clue as to what was going on.

"I'll check the bureau drawers," Cassie said as soon as he switched it on. She started around the side of the bed toward the bureau, then suddenly stopped. She gulped as an icy chill slithered over her skin.

"What is it?" Dan swung the flashlight around the room at waist level. The room appeared empty.

"Exit one suspect," she murmured, pointing a shaking finger at the body lying sprawled on the floor between the bed and the wall.

"Here. Hold this." Dan shoved the flashlight at her as he pushed past her. Reluctantly, he rolled Smith on his back and pressed his hand against the vein in his neck, searching for a pulse. At first the pounding of his own heart drowned out all other sensations, but finally he was able to make out a thin, thready beat.

Cassie took a deep breath, trying to control her panicky urge to scream and then run like hell. "Is he . . ."

"No. At least not yet. Shine that light down here so I can see what happened."

Cassie did so obediently and then wished she hadn't. Her stomach lurched in protest at the sight of the congealed blood on Smith's abused temple.

"What happened to him?" she asked.

Dan slowly got to his feet. "At a guess, I'd say that he ran into the proverbial blunt instrument."

"But if he isn't the assassin, then who. . ." Cassie found it hard to give him up as the villain.

"Who is?" Dan finished for her. "I don't know, but—"

"Well, well, what have we here?"

Cassie whirled around at the unexpected sound of another voice, blinking as her eyes struggled to adjust to the bright light coming from the camping lantern Madam Rowinski was holding in her hand—in her left hand. One part of Cassie's mind cataloged the fact. In the woman's right was a very large, black pistol.

Cassie felt herself relax slightly. They were no longer unarmed. "Madam Rowinski, did you see whoever did this to poor Mr. Smith?" she asked.

"Yes." The humor in the medium's voice struck Cassie as curiously inappropriate. "I did."

Cassie blinked uncertainly. "You mean he threatened you and you—"

"I think she means she's the hit man," Dan said, his voice calm, though his mind was frantically weighing the options open to him. He couldn't let this woman harm Cassie. No matter what happened to him, he simply couldn't allow Cassie to be hurt. But if he was to have any chance of disarming Madam Rowinski, he had to get closer. At this distance he'd never be able to get the gun away from her before she killed the both of them. If he could just keep her talking...

"Hit man!" Cassie repeated in shocked disbelief. "Madam Rowinski? What self-respecting woman would hire herself out to murder people?"

"One whose husband was a very improvident provider."
Madam Rowinski shrugged. "Believe me, there's nothing
personal in it, Miss Whitney. I really rather like you, but you
must see that I can't leave any witnesses behind."

"She's serious!" Incredulously, Cassie turned to Dan.
"The woman actually kills people for money."

"For lots of money," Madam Rowinski corrected.

"You disabled the lights?" Dan asked, stalling for time.

"Child's play. You never even suspected me. He didn't,
either." She nodded contemptuously toward Smith's limp
body.

Cassie swallowed at the metallic taste of fear that coated
her mouth. She couldn't believe this. She was about to die
at the hands of a woman who looked like the quintessential
grandmother. And Dan... For a moment panic gained the
upper hand, making her feel faint. She was going to loose
Dan. That single stark fact extinguished her panic, leaving
in its wake a vast void of despair. After thirty-four years,
she'd finally found the man she loved, the man who had
been created to be her other half, and she was going to loose
him. To loose him before she'd ever really had him. She
struggled to control her ragged breathing.

She stole a quick glance at Dan, to find him staring at the
huge gun Madam Rowinski was holding. He was going to
try to take it away from her; the knowledge burst into her
mind. And when he tried, she would shoot him.

But if she could distract Madam Rowinski, draw her
fire... Cassie's frantic thoughts ricocheted through her
mind. Perhaps Dan would have time to wrestle the gun away
from her before she could fire a second time. Then he would
be safe.

The thought steadied her nerves somewhat. If she
couldn't have Dan, then she didn't really care if she were
dead or alive. And that being the case, she might as well try
to save him.

"Since you're going to kill us anyway, at least satisfy my curiosity." Dan tried to keep her talking. "Why the amateurish games with the poison and the brakes on the car?"

"Greed," Madam Rowinski said succinctly. "There was a bonus if I could make it look like an accident. I left the kid's slingshot by the poison, hoping he'd be blamed."

"Why?" Cassie asked, trying not to let her eyes stray to Dan.

"Buczek wants Travis dead, but he would prefer that there be a little ambiguity about how he died. Buczek's afraid a jury might be influenced if he'd hired a hit man."

"But they'll know he did if you shoot us," Cassie pointed out.

"My instructions were precise. Buczek wants Travis dead more than he's worried about the jury. Now then, I don't know what time the old lady's getting back, and since it would pain me to have to kill her, too..."

"If'n you don't beat the Dutch!" Jonas' incredulous voice came from the other side of the room.

Dan took a quick step toward Madam Rowinski, only to come to a precipitous halt when she pointed the gun at Cassie.

"You move and she dies first." Madam Rowinski's voice was all the more frightening for its total lack of emotion. "This just means I'll have to use one more bullet. I swear," she said in exasperation, "I should be getting that bonus for all the trouble this hit has been."

"It's what comes of giving women the vote," Jonas pronounced as he started toward her.

Madam Rowinski aimed at him and calmly pulled the trigger. A deafening roar echoed through the small room.

Cassie closed her eyes as the full enormity of what had just happened ripped through her mind. Madam Rowinski had actually shot poor Jonas, who'd never harmed a soul.

"Now he really is a ghost," Madam Rowinski said, sounding amused.

"Always was a ghost," Jonas corrected, and Cassie swung around, staring at him in disbelief. How had Madam Rowinski missed him at that range? she wondered in confusion.

"What the hell? I shot you!" Madam Rowinski's hand shook slightly, and Cassie watched the wavering gun in morbid fascination. Should she try to distract her now or wait and see if the supposed medium became more rattled?

As Cassie frantically weighed her options, Jonas calmly removed his head, turned it around on his hands and seemed to stare at it. Cassie tried to assimilate this totally unexpected development. His eyes were in his head and his head appeared to be in his hands!

"I think you've damaged my left eye," Jonas said accusingly. "Look." He strode toward Madam Rowinski, holding his head out in front of him.

"Stand back!" the woman screamed, and she fired again.

Dan, figuring he'd never get a better chance, lunged at her. He caught her around her ample waist and knocked her backward. Her head hit the doorframe with a crack and she sagged limply against it, slowly slipping to the floor.

Dan yanked the gun out of her lax fingers.

"Jonas!" Cassie scrambled for her flashlight and swung it around the room, terrified of what she would find. "He saved us, Dan," she sobbed. "Jonas saved us."

"Yes, I did, didn't I?" To Cassie's incalculable relief, Jonas got to his feet from the other side of the bed. His head was now firmly back on his shoulders, where it belonged. "Would you say that that was a good deed?" he asked.

"Best damn good deed I ever saw," Dan feverently agreed.

"Along with the best trick I've ever seen," Cassie said in congratulations. "How did you do that with your head, and why didn't her bullet hit you? Are you wearing a flak jacket? Are you really from the Justice Department, sent to guard Dan?"

"First we tie Madam Rowinski up and then we can discuss the tricks of Jonas' trade," Dan ordered, looking around for something to use.

Cassie picked up the boning knife she'd dropped. "Her room has venetian blinds. I'll cut the cords and we can use them," she said as she rushed out.

Dan slumped against the wall as a feeling of release seemed to render him boneless. Just minutes ago he'd felt as if his whole life were ending and now...now he suddenly had a future filled with endless promise. Warmth began to seep into his frozen body. If he could just convince Cassie to share it with him.

"Here." She hurried back with two lengths of thin cord dangling from her fingers. "And look what I found." She held something up with a triumphant grin.

Dan squinted at the rectangular object through the dim light. "A portable phone?"

"Yup. Our hit...person had it lying on her bed."

Cassie plopped down on Smith's bed and dialed 911 while Dan efficiently tied up Madam Rowinski.

"There." He tested the knots. "That should hold her until the police get here."

"Where'd Jonas go?" Cassie asked as she switched the phone off.

"Jonas?" Dan frowned at the empty space between the bed and the window. "He was here a minute ago."

Cassie chuckled. "He probably went down to the kitchen to fortify himself after his ordeal. That trick with his head was the neatest thing I've ever seen. I hope it isn't some kind of magician's professional secret, because I want to learn how to do it. It...what's the matter?" she asked.

Dan was still staring at the spot where Jonas had been standing. "He couldn't have gone down to the kitchen because the only way out of this room is through the door, and I was in front of it, guarding Madam Rowinski."

Cassie glanced around the room. "Well, if he didn't leave, he must still be here."

"I didn't say he didn't leave," Dan said slowly. "I said he didn't go out through the door."

"Maybe he's in the bathroom or the closet. Maybe reaction set in and the poor man's fainted."

Dan obediently shone the flashlight into the narrow closet and the small bath. Both cubicles were clearly empty.

"He disappeared just like that the *first* time I ever saw him," he muttered. "I assumed that he climbed off the roof, but... Tell me, Cassie, what do you really know about him?"

Cassie opened her mouth and then closed it as she suddenly realized that the only thing she knew about Jonas for certain was that he was a shrewd judge of character and had a voracious appetite.

She stared at Dan, her eyes slowly widening as an incredible idea occurred to her. She shook her head in negation of it.

"No," she said emphatically. "I don't believe in ghosts. They don't exist."

Dan grimaced. "I don't, either, but..."

"Jonas must have come from the Justice Department," Cassie said. "They probably sent him to keep an eye on you."

"We didn't tell the Justice Department where I was going because we were afraid of leaks," Dan said, scotching her theory.

"But Jonas is a very nice, down-on-his-luck actor," Cassie insisted. "Ghosts are always portrayed as nasty, vicious predators who scare people."

"He did a damned good job of scaring her." Dan pointed to Madam Rowinski, who was starting to stir.

"But if he'd given her what she deserved, she'd be the ghost." Cassie glared at the woman, feeling no sympathy when she moaned. Madam Rowinski had tried to kill the man she loved and for that Cassie would never forgive her.

Dan sighed. "One thing my years in journalism has taught me is that criminals rarely get what they deserve. I'll give you odds that she'll be back on the street in two years."

Cassie echoed his sigh. "You're probably right. I wish that ambulance would get here." She glanced worriedly at Smith, who was still lying there, oblivious to the whole traumatic mess. "Much as I'd like to put her away for good, I don't want to have to use Smith's death as the cause."

"Ah, I hear the cavalry now." Dan pulled aside the curtain and peered out, watching as the flashing red lights of an ambulance and the sheriff's patrol car turned off the cliff road toward the inn.

"I'll go let them in. You keep track of Lucretia Borgia there." Cassie hurried down to meet the authorities.

In a surprisingly short space of time, the police had carted Madam Rowinski away and Smith had been carefully loaded into the ambulance by an encouraging young doctor from the local hospital, who had assured them he'd be just fine. He told them that the human head was a lot harder than most people gave it credit for.

"And that, as they say, is that," Cassie muttered as she closed the door behind them and sagged against it. Her energy suddenly seemed to drain out of her now that the danger was past.

"Not quite." Dan stared intently at her. "I'm not sure how this should be done." He glanced around the lobby, which was inadequately lit by the light from Madam Rowinski's lantern. "We need to fix the lights."

"No—Sam, the electrician, needs to fix the lights. I haven't the vaguest idea what that blasted woman did to them, and I have no intention of finishing off the evening by electrocuting one or both of us. The sheriff said he'd call Sam and ask him to come out as soon as he booked Madam Rowinski.

"Actually—" Cassie looked around at the shadows pushing in at the edges of the lantern light "—I think it's kind of romantic." Now that she knew they were safe, the dark was no longer sinister and frightening. It was friendly and welcoming.

"The Black Hole of Calcutta would be romantic with you."

"Thank you. I think," Cassie muttered, studying him uncertainly. Dan was clearly agitated, and some of his obvious nervousness was beginning to dampen her sense of euphoric release. Was he trying to find the words to say goodbye now that the danger was over? Now that he was able to return to his normal life? If flitting around the world chasing natural and man-made disasters could be called normal, that is.

Had she merely been a temporary diversion to keep his mind off his troubles? Now that his troubles were over and he was about to return to wherever it was he normally went, maybe he didn't want to leave any unfinished business behind.

Cassie felt her skin tighten with the pain of his anticipated rejection. She couldn't bear the thought of him leaving. Not now. Not after what they'd shared. But how could she stop him? Short of tying him up in the basement, she couldn't, she thought hopelessly. Dan was a grown man. He had to make his own choices. Simply because her feelings for him bordered on idolatry didn't mean that he saw her as anything more than a congenial partner for a vacation fling.

Her mind screamed in denial at the very thought that that was all she'd been, and she clenched her jaws together to keep back the hasty words clamoring to escape. She didn't want him to leave with the memory of her begging him not to. She wanted him to remember her as a mature woman who hadn't tried to manipulate him with tears and recriminations. That way he might come back. He might visit her between pestilences and famines and wars. If all she could share with him was an occasional weekend dodging bullets from angry mobsters, she'd take it. Accept it gratefully and cherish every moment.

"Yes?" she prodded, wanting to get it over with. She wasn't sure just how long her brave front would last.

"Oh, what the hell!" Dan gestured impotently. "I might as well try the traditional route."

To Cassie's utter amazement, he suddenly dropped to one knee and said, "Cassie Whitney, will you marry me?"

When she stared at him, shocked into silence by something she hadn't expected and was afraid to believe she'd really heard, he added, "Please. I love you to distraction, you know."

"You do?" she asked hesitantly.

"Of course I do." His voice developed an edge. "Why else do you think I'm kneeling here like an extra in a French farce?"

"Oh, Dan!" Cassie flung herself at him. He reached up in time to catch her, but the weight of her body overbalanced him and they sprawled on the Oriental carpet. She didn't care. Nothing mattered but that Dan had said he loved her. And if he'd said it, he meant it. He wasn't the kind of man to lie.

"Is that a yes or a no?" he asked cautiously.

"Yes, yes and yes! I love you, love you, love you!" She punctuated each word with a kiss.

"You do?" He crushed her pliant body against his chest.

"Of course I do." She wiggled slightly, sighing happily as his body immediately reacted.

"Don't do that. I want to talk to you."

"But, Dan—" she wiggled again "—thinking is not what you do best, and as an advertising executive, I can tell you that people should always exploit their strong points."

"Yes." Dan's eyes narrowed thoughtfully as he remembered his earlier plan. "I was thinking about that."

"Hmm?" Cassie nuzzled his ear with her lips, breathing deeply of his delicious masculine scent. "I think about that all the time."

He chuckled. "That, too. But what I was actually referring to was your job."

Cassie raised her head and peered down into his guarded eyes in confusion. "You don't like my job?"

"No, that's not it. It's my job I don't like," he said harshly. "It almost got us both killed tonight, and I'm tired of it. I want a normal life. I want to come home every night and be mobbed by my kids, and maybe a dog or two. I want to be able to make mad, passionate love to my wife every night."

"Sounds great to me." Cassie felt a warm glow of happiness at the image his words provoked. "But what's that got to do with my job?"

"I..." He paused uncertainly. "If you were willing to leave Welton and Mitchell, we could buy the paper from Ed, and I could do the news and you could run the advertising," he finally blurted out.

"What a fantastic idea!" Cassie rained kisses on his face. "I moved to New York in the first place only because there were no jobs in advertising here, and Levington is the perfect place to raise a family, and I know the company will let me handle all the free-lance work for them I want and—" She broke off as the door suddenly opened to reveal her aunt, flanked by two other elderly ladies.

Cassie winced and would have scooted off Dan, but his arms tightened protestingly.

Hannah peered down at them in surprise. "In my day, young man, gentlemen had far more imagination than to use the floor of the front hallway for their romantic trysts."

"Not always, Hannah," the pudgy little woman beside her disagreed. "Remember Oscar Everton and the time he—"

"Forget Oscar, Jessie," Aunt Hannah ordered.

"It isn't Dan's fault," Cassie said, defending him. "He was down on one knee proposing to me, and I flung myself at him and overbalanced him."

"And you said modern men had no sense of romance, Hannah," Chloe, on Hannah's other side, said reprovingly.

"I was wrong," Hannah admitted fairly. "Cassie's young man is very romantic. He is also going to be rather dusty."

Cassie scrambled off him, keeping a firm hold on one of his hands. She almost felt as if, were she to let go of him, it might all turn out to be a dream.

Dan awkwardly got to his feet and pulled Cassie against his side.

"Do you know where those police cars we passed on the cliff road were coming from?" Jessie asked avidly.

Cassie looked at Dan and, at his helpless shrug, grimaced. Much as she would prefer to keep the whole thing from her aunt, there was no way she could. Not in a small town like Levington.

"Actually, they were coming from here, and only one of them was a police car. The other was an ambulance."

Chloe wrung her hands in dread. "Who died?"

Dan felt his stomach do a flip-flop as he realized that if it hadn't been for Jonas, the answer could well have been he and Cassie. It would have been their lifeless bodies the ambulance carried away. His arm tightened convulsively, and Cassie snuggled comfortingly against his side.

"No one," she soothed. "The ambulance was for Mr. Smith. He had a bump on his head."

"He hit it?" Aunt Hannah frowned worriedly.

"No, someone hit it for him," Cassie muttered, trying to decide what was the best way to tell her aunt that they'd been harboring a cold-blooded killer.

"Not you, I hope?" Jessie looked sternly at Cassie.

"Oh no," Cassie disclaimed. "Madam Rowinski did."

"Why would she do a thing like that?" Aunt Hannah got the question in before Jessie could.

"So she could kill me," Dan said.

"Mercy!" Chloe peered at him in horror.

"She was a hit man hired by a gangster Dan wrote about," Cassie elaborated.

"That is carrying job equality entirely too far!" Aunt Hannah said disapprovingly. "Does this mean that we can expect another attempt?"

"No," Dan assured her. "While the police were removing Madam Rowinski, I finally got hold of my editor to tell him what happened to Smith, and he told me that the gangster after me was gunned down in a restaurant this afternoon. Fortunately, his successor has no interest in me whatsoever. So we're safe."

Jessie shook her head in mournful satisfaction. "It's just like the Good Book says. He who lives by the sword will die by the sword."

"And Dan is going to buy the newspaper from Ed, and we're going to live right here in Levington," Cassie announced. "I'll be able to help you with the inn whenever you need me."

Hannah cleared her throat and looked uncertainly at the other two ladies. "Your coming home where you belong is good news of course, but... actually, dear, I am going to close the inn."

Cassie blinked, remembering how hard she'd tried to convince her aunt to do just that. Tried and failed. Had this latest fiasco finally convinced her?

"You see, we couldn't get the judge to issue an injunction to stop that builder from tearing down our apartment building," Jessie elaborated.

"Yes?" Cassie asked, not making the connection.

"So the three of us talked it over, and Chloe and I are going to rent rooms here from Hannah," Jessie announced. "That way we'll have a nice home we can afford, and Hannah will have company and enough money to pay the taxes and the heating bill.''

"Cassie and I would be more than happy to pay your bills," Dan offered, and received a reproving glare for his effort.

"Thank you, young man, but as I explained to Cassie, I prefer my independence. Plenty of time for you to pay the taxes when I'm dead and gone and the house is yours. Come along, girls," Hannah ordered. "I think we should give the young couple some privacy while we fix coffee." She picked up the lantern and headed toward the kitchen, but turned back as she suddenly remembered something.

"By the way, dear, I ran into Moira Featheringham, and she said she was sorry that she hadn't been able to find anyone to handle our role as ghost."

"But if she didn't send Jonas..." Cassie swallowed uneasily. "Then where did he come from?"

"I don't know, dear. Perhaps he heard about the job from someone she did ask. Anyway, when you see him, tell him we won't need him to haunt the inn anymore, but he's welcome to help with the gardens until he can find something else." With a nod, she disappeared into the kitchen, followed by her two friends, each of whom bestowed an approving nod on Cassie and Dan as they passed.

Cassie watched the door swing shut behind them and then turned to Dan. "Dan, you don't think that—"

"There are no such things as ghosts," he insisted. "And there also isn't much time. If I read my little old ladies right, they'll be back here with coffee and cookies inside of ten minutes."

Cassie reached up and took his beloved face between her hands. A slow, seductive smile curved her lips. "Then let's not waste a second," she said as she pulled his lips down to meet hers.

"Perfect!" Jonas pronounced from his perch on the roof. "Yes, perfect." Millicent echoed his sentiment. "I must say, Jonas Middlebury, when you put your mind to it, you get results. Even Saint Peter was impressed." She shyly inched nearer to him.

To her pleasure, his arm crept around her thin waist and he pulled her closer still.

"Yes," she repeated. "All heaven wanted was one good deed, and you saved three lives, brought a very nasty person to justice and made a match, too." Greatly daring, Millicent stroked the side of Jonas' cheek.

"For you, my precious, anything," Jonas claimed. And taking his clue from the oblivious couple below, he kissed his beloved Millicent. He found it worth all the trouble he'd been put through.

\* \* \* \* \*